D0034997

Also by Maureen Lipinski

Shadow's Edge

Funded by LSTA Grant
BOOKS4U PROJECT
2013

CLEOPATRA ASCENDING

A Shadow's Edge Novel

CLEOPATRA ASCENDING

Maureen Lipinski

flux

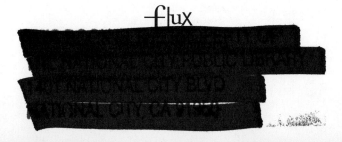

NOV 13

Cleopatra Ascending © 2013 by Maureen Lipinski. All rights reserved. No part of this book may be used or reproduced in any manner whatsoever, including Internet usage, without written permission from Flux, except in the case of brief quotations embodied in critical articles and reviews.

First Edition
First Printing, 2013

Book design by Bob Gaul
Cover design by Lisa Novak
Cover images: Background © iStockphoto.com/
              The Power of Forever Photography
              Woman © Subbotina Anna/Shutterstock Images LLC
Interior ankh art © Llewellyn art department

Flux, an imprint of Llewellyn Worldwide Ltd.

This is a work of fiction. Names, characters, places, and incidents are either the product of the author's imagination or are used fictitiously, and any resemblance to actual persons living or dead, business establishments, events, or locales is entirely coincidental. Cover model used for illustrative purposes only and may not endorse or represent the book's subject.

Library of Congress Cataloging-in-Publication Data
Lipinski, Maureen.
  Cleopatra ascending/Maureen Lipinski.—First edition.
     pages cm.—(A Shadow's edge novel; #2)
  Summary: Despite living with a shaman, a witch, and a muse for sisters, Rhea feels like a normal teenager—even if she is the reincarnation of Cleopatra—until she turns sixteen and must travel to Egypt to stop the Octavians from accessing the magic deep below the desert sands.
  ISBN 978-0-7387-3193-3
[1. Magic—Fiction. 2. High schools—Fiction. 3. Schools—Fiction. 4. Sisters—Fiction. 5. Supernatural—Fiction.] I. Title.
  PZ7.L66366Cl 2013
  [Fic]—dc23
                                                2012033960

                            Flux
                  Llewellyn Worldwide Ltd.
                    2143 Wooddale Drive
                  Woodbury, MN 55125-2989
                      www.fluxnow.com

Printed in the United States of America

For Ryan and Paige

PROLOGUE

Cleopatra stared at the basket of figs... there was a deadly asp hidden below the fruit. All she had to do was place her hand inside and it would all be over. She knew she had no other choice. Octavian's army was literally knocking at the door of her mausoleum, her kingdom was about to fall to Rome, and she would soon be paraded through the streets in gilded chains like a captured animal.

And Mark Antony—her life, love, and everything else in between—was dead.

Iras and Charmian, her ladies-in-waiting, stood at their queen's side, questioning. They had been with her throughout her long reign—through the endless struggles with her brother Ptolemy, her relationships with Julius Caesar and Mark Antony, and countless perils. Cleopatra had tried to wave them off when Octavian's army advanced to capture her, but they remained with her. As they continued to do now, even through this last choice.

The queen adjusted the white ribbon on her head—her diadem—as she slowly picked up a fig and twirled it around.

There had been so many years of fighting, of negotiating, of…winning. To think it should all end like this, in this room with gold-dripped paintings, while the country crumbled around her. She could continue the fight, certainly, but it would mean the deaths of thousands of her people, and she wasn't willing to see any more Egyptian bloodshed. She couldn't watch as wives wept over their husband's bodies and children cried out for fathers who would never return. If she fought, some of her people could be taken as slaves.

"My lady?" Iras asked her. The asp underneath the figs was beginning to wake up. It stared at them with two diamond yellow and black eyes, ready to bite.

Cleopatra sighed heavily, closed her eyes, and nodded. She didn't watch as Iras picked up the snake, but she did hear the woman's strangled scream as the asp bit her. When Cleopatra opened her eyes, she saw her fair lady-in-waiting crumpled on the ground, gasping for air.

Charmian started to walk toward the snake, now slowly slithering across the marble floor. Cleopatra placed a hand on her shoulder. "Let me go next. That way, you can be sure

I am properly positioned." Charmian nodded and bowed her head slowly.

Cleopatra gazed out the small square window at the Mediterranean in the distance. When the country she loved fell to Rome, it would become just another one of their territories. The people she'd protected for so long would be vulnerable.

And there was nothing she could do about it.

Except this. She could escape with some dignity and join her true love in the afterlife. They would meet Octavian again in the next life—and that time, they would be victorious.

Her eyes fixed on a golden box adorned with pearls and jewels that sat near the window.

"It will be safe forever, Queen. Throughout this life and all others," Charmian whispered. "We have already arranged for its safe transport."

"Then there is nothing left to do," Cleopatra said. She slowly picked up the writhing snake, pulled the collar of her robe down, and placed the snake on her chest.

She felt it bite her, a white-hot pain that rushed through her body. Her legs went numb and she crumpled against the brocade couch in the room.

"May the gods have mercy on me. And may we claim victory in the future," she whispered in Egyptian.

The queen slowly closed her eyes, and with her death, Egypt fell.

A dust storm blew across the desert that night, across the room as they prepared Cleopatra's tomb, across the golden box that would not dare whisper any secrets.

ONE

For as long as I could remember, I looked forward to turning sixteen. I figured sixteen would be the magical year when I would get my license, be treated like an adult in my family, and finally stop having to sit at the kids' table on holidays. I'm not sure why I picked that age—in fact, it seems kind of arbitrary—but I was sure my sixteenth year would bring fabulous new gifts and surprises.

As it turned out, I was right.

Except, instead of attending some fantastic party thrown by my friends or driving around in some great new car with a big red bow, I was gifted with trash. Piles and piles of trash.

"Queen Rhea, you'd better take that garbage out now," my sister Leah said as she stretched her arms over her head. She was sitting on the blue-and-white gingham couch in our family room, her boyfriend Ben at her side. She peered down at me, crossing her arms over her chest, as I lay on the floor watching television.

I rolled my eyes. As the third out of four sisters, I was forever being "reminded" to do my chores. "I'm busy," I said. I tried to muster up a fantastical power, such as the ability to turn household objects into little slaves, like in those Disney movies.

No such luck.

"You better finish it before Mom comes home," Leah said. I shot her a dirty look while Ben shifted uncomfortably. I would've felt bad for him, but he should be used to uncomfortable situations—Leah can be such a dork sometimes.

But I knew she was right. Mom was probably at the grocery store right now, pausing to stare at a display of red peppers and disapprovingly shaking her head at my laziness. When it comes to sneaking things past my mom, I've always been at a serious disadvantage. She's a famous psychic whose spirit guides tell her everything, including the disobedient things my sisters and I do behind her back. Sometimes having a special mom is less than fun.

In fact, my entire family is kind of "special." My older sisters Morgana and Leah are, respectively, a Witch who conducts energy healings and a Shaman to the Other Realm. My younger sister Gia is a Muse.

I glanced at Leah, stood up, and sighed loudly. "Happy birthday to me." I'd been sixteen all of a few hours so far, and my year wasn't shaping up to be any better than the previous fifteen.

"It's your own fault you're stuck inside today. If you hadn't broken curfew—again—you wouldn't be grounded on your birthday." Leah cocked her head back and forth, mocking me.

"I'm aware of that, thanks." I shot her another look before heading into the kitchen to take the last bag of trash out. Lucky for me, Morgana's cat, Doppler, had barfed all over the floor and she'd filled up the bag with cat-puke paper towels. I again wished for powers like my sisters had, instead of the warped, strange gift I was given.

Or, should I say, was born with.

When my mom was pregnant with me, she had a dream that I was a queen. I had a large pearl and gold scepter in my hand and a tall, striped crown made of onyx on my head. Based on this, my mom said, she knew I was destined for greatness. Little did she know that it was more like I'd been *previously* destined for greatness. Just before I was born, she had another dream, and this time she saw exactly what name I used to have:

Cleopatra.

I am Cleopatra, reincarnated.

At first, this might sound really special and different— but trust me, it never afforded me any special treatment in life or at home. I'm a former Egyptian queen … who had to spend her sixteenth birthday cleaning out the garage and taking out the trash.

I grabbed the slimy garbage bag from the kitchen and hauled it outside. As I closed the lid on the can, I sighed. It was a warm night, almost June, just before school got out for the summer, and a perfect time to hang out with my friends. They were likely at Ali Erickson's house, blasting music and swimming in her pool that had a waterfall. Her parents only rule was, don't come in the house and bother us and we won't bother you.

I looked up at the sky, wishing once again that I hadn't come home so late the previous week. It really wasn't my fault. It was my friend Harper's fault. Her car got a flat tire on the way home from the movie, but my parents didn't care about the reason and grounded me anyway.

"Star light, star bright..." I started to whisper up at the sky, then stopped. "Whoa." I sucked my breath in and craned my neck around. The clear night sky was filled with so many twinkling stars that I seemed to be looking at glittery, milky streaks. One star in particular seemed to twinkle pink, straight above my head. I vaguely remembered hearing something on the news about one particular star being closer to Earth than it had been in hundreds of years.

"There's more trash in here! I almost stepped on a banana peel," Leah called from the house.

"Maybe you should just pick it up yourself," I grumbled under my breath.

I tore my eyes away from the stars and shot a dirty look toward my house. We live in a small brick two-story Colonial with a deck off the back. Our backyard is average-sized, but Leah claims most of it for her Other Realm duties, so we have all these miniature gardens and platforms that she uses to communicate with Other Realm beings. I suggested our backyard would be better served by a swimming pool, but once again I got outvoted. So instead of a beautiful, sparkling lagoon there are small toadstools, offering platters, and tiny purple doorways to the Other Realm.

"You better not be trying to sneak out!" Leah yelled.

I trudged toward the house, muttering under my breath. Despite having three sisters, two parents, and one neurotic cat, I seemed to be the only one on indentured servant duty. Ever. I'm sure in my aristocratic past I had servants for everything and never had to wipe spilled coffee grounds off the floor.

As I came inside, I heard Ben clicking through the TV channels; he stopped on the nightly news. Normally I don't watch the news, but one word make me freeze—and made my ears practically turn around like the cat's whenever she hears the words "eat" and "catnip."

Cleopatra.

"Ben, stop," I heard Leah say. I slid across the kitchen, into the family room. And yes, I tripped over the banana peel. Leah and I briefly locked eyes as I planted myself in front of the television, my hands on my hips.

The story began with a video clip of a desert presumably somewhere in Egypt. Men in white robes stood around with shovels and sifting platters while a guy wearing a blue shirt and khaki pants wiped his head with a bandana. The news anchor's voiceover said, "Archaeologists think they are close to finding the location of Cleopatra's tomb in Egypt. Lost for centuries, the Egyptian queen's burial site has never been uncovered, despite intense searching."

The guy in khaki pants, an American identified as Paul Coburn, said, "Uncovering such a treasure would be invaluable for the field of antiquities, not to mention the historical significance of the artifacts that are certainly buried with Cleopatra. We have already unearthed many treasures from her time, and finding her tomb would far surpass the finding of King Tut's tomb. It would rightly be considered the greatest archaeological discovery in history."

The news anchor came back on. "Officials say that they are digging near Taposiris Magna, an area close to Alexandria. Deep passageways have been found that Coburn believes lead to a mausoleum possibly containing the remains of the great queen. The crew hopes to soon reach the inner sanctum. Experts say that there may be artifacts of priceless value in the tomb."

Leah cleared her throat but I refused to turn around and look at her. The news switched over to a story about a bird that ate a woman's engagement ring. I stayed still, hands pressed to my sides. I felt a trickle of sweat run down my back.

What does this mean?

Is this a good thing or a bad thing or a ... who cares thing?

"Rhea?" Leah said.

I slowly turned around and shrugged my shoulders. "That's interesting. It would be cool to see where she's buried and I'm sure it would be a big tourist attraction, but I don't think it has anything to do with me."

Ben shifted uncomfortably again and pretended to study the remote control. He's a "regular" guy, and although he knows all about our family, he sometimes acts like he thinks we're all possessed. I've told him not to worry—if he ever got possessed, Morgana would fix him. But he didn't seem comforted by that fact.

Leah kept staring at me. "Do you think we should tell Mom about this?" she asked.

"If you want. Go ahead." I glanced toward the kitchen meaningfully. "Think it'll get me off garbage duty? After all, Cleopatra had servants or slaves to help *her*."

Leah rolled her eyes. "Not likely."

Sighing, I walked back into the kitchen and casually started gathering up the leftover pizza boxes, but my hands were shaking slightly. I walked outside with the trash and shivered, despite the warm air.

" ... coming for you ... " I heard the slightest whisper in the air.

I whirled around. "Hello? Who's there?"

Then I realized that I sounded exactly like one of those dumb girls in horror movies who falls while the killer is chasing her. Which always makes me start rooting for her to get offed based on her stupidity. I mean, no one's boyfriend hides in the woods and whispers threats, so don't go check it out, okay?

"I'm hearing things now. Great," I muttered to myself as I quickly walked back into the house. Yet as I stepped inside, my footing wobbled, and I realized the floor was covered with sand.

Sand was everywhere, pouring out of the cabinets in the kitchen, filling the room.

"Leah?" I shouted, but the sand was piling up around my waist, trapping me. It choked my mouth and went up my nose until I couldn't move. I was buried under the sand with just my head sticking out. It all happened so quickly, I didn't even have time to panic.

Until I saw a black and brown snake, about twenty feet away, start to move slowly across the sand. It was heading straight for my face.

I screamed and tried to thrash my way out of the sand, but I couldn't move at all. It was like I was stuck in concrete.

"Please, no," I whimpered as the snake stopped in front of me. It slowly opened its mouth and I saw that its razor-sharp fangs were dripping with venom.

The snake paused and hissed. And then the fangs flew toward my face.

I closed my eyes and screamed, bracing for searing pain. Instead, I felt a hand on my arm.

"Rhea! What's wrong?" Leah shook me hard.

I looked around and saw that I was standing in the kitchen. I must've ... dreamt it, hallucinated, blacked out. Something.

"Sand. There was sand," I sputtered. I looked down at the floor, but it was just regular linoleum, with no sign of any reptiles.

"What?"

"Nothing. I—nothing." I took a deep breath and tried to steady my heartbeat.

"Should I call Mom and Dad? You don't look well." Leah narrowed her eyes at me and I could tell she was wondering if I had some great master scheme in motion.

"I'm great." I shook free of my sister and ran toward my bedroom.

It was a dream. A daydream. A really messed-up daydream, I thought as I sat on my bed. I steadied my breathing and pushed my hair out of my eyes. Lots of strange things happened in my house, thanks to my family's gifts, and I was certain that it was just another strange apparition or happening.

"I just need a good night's sleep," I said firmly.

Yet as I kicked off my shoes, tiny grains of sand spilled out onto the carpet.

TWO

I didn't have any more visions the week after my birthday. Despite my strange encounter with the sand-snake, life went on in the most predictable way. I went to school each day, became nauseous in the cafeteria about the gross hot lunch, hid in the back of the class during Trig, and dropped part of my homework as I left the building on Friday afternoon.

"Damn it," I muttered as my history notebook hit the sidewalk outside Westerville High. My notes on the American Revolution went scattering past a group of kids smoking cigarettes and laughing at a prom banner.

Oh well.

It's not like my notes were that great anyway. After the whole sand-eating daydream, I hadn't really been able to concentrate. In fact, I'd spent most of that day's history class thinking about how George Washington really could've gotten a better-looking wife than Martha. I mean, he was George. Washington. And Martha was, well, let's just say, not a Ten. Even in butter-churning times.

Thankfully, in a couple weeks the school year would be over and I would have three long months to practice my eye/hand coordination.

I slung my black messenger bag across my chest and started to walk home. I wanted to get a head start before Leah could catch up with me. I was the only sister who went to Westerville High with her, so she kind of thought it was her goddess-given duty to watch out for me. Morgana and Gia were homeschooled, like I'd been when we moved to Westerville last fall and Leah decided to give the regular high school thing a whirl. It seemed pretty interesting, so in January, I signed myself up too. Needless to say, my mom wasn't happy, since she'd prefer that we stay home and study things like homeopathy and music healing, instead of geometry and chemistry.

I turned onto the sidewalk and walked through neighborhoods that look straight out of a television show; most of the houses are two-story brick Colonials like ours. From what I've gathered so far, the moms in Westerville stay home with their kids, join the PTA, and organize bake sales while the dads are at work. I'm sure dinner is on the table by six o'clock and no one ever has to set a place for their mom's spirit guide.

I took my usual route home, pretending to be oblivious as the heads turned in my direction. I always seem to attract attention wherever I go, something my mom says is due to my reincarnation powers but which I always just say is because I can accessorize fantastically. I usually tried to shrug off any discussions about Cleopatra and what exactly it might mean to be her spirit reincarnated. Truth was, it both thrilled and creeped me out a little to know this was my second go-round on this earth. Mainly, I guess, because it didn't really make any sense—like, what was the point? And it wasn't like my history textbook had the answers.

I felt a hand on my shoulder and my bare skin tingled. I knew exactly who it was.

"Hey," I said without turning around.

He placed his other hand on my other shoulder, and I turned around.

"Miss me?" I asked, looking up—way up, since he's almost 6′5—at my boyfriend Slade. His black hair hung longish and shaggy against his dark face and he was dressed in his typical uniform—a black T-shirt and black pants.

"Of course," he said. He leaned down and kissed me. Shivers ran down my legs, just like they always did.

I opened my eyes and saw that a crowd of my classmates was staring at us from across the street. *I better get out of here before Leah sees us and demands we keep a four-foot distance between us at all times.* "Let's keep walking," I said quickly, as I grabbed Slade's T-shirt and pulled him down the block. Once we were safely away from any curious glances, we slowed down.

"I want to ask you something," Slade said as he shoved his hands into his pockets. "My parents want to meet you." He pronounced each word slowly and painfully, punctuating them with a scowl at the end.

I threw my head back and laughed. His parents. Hilarious. But when I looked at him, I noticed that his dark eyes had changed into a lighter shade of amber. Oops. He was serious.

"Sure. I mean, yeah. Definitely. I would love to meet them," I said.

His eyes quickly changed back to their usual blue-black, and he nodded.

Normally, someone's eyes changing color would freak me out. However, Slade isn't ... typical. He's actually a Créatúir. A shapeshifter, if you want to get technical. I met him nine months ago when he and Leah were solving a murder spree in the Créatúir world. Eventually my sisters and I had to get involved and we wound up epically battling the Créatúir's enemies—the Fomoriian demons—on a not-so-average Saturday night. The reason Slade first came by our house was to make sure Leah was doing her Shaman duties, but then the two of us actually started hanging out. In the beginning, his differences just intrigued me, but as I got to know him better as a person—I use that term loosely, obviously—I discovered that we're actually more alike than I could've imagined.

So, needless to say, I knew that meeting his parents wouldn't be the usual pot-roast-dinner kind of introduction. Which, I supposed, was fine, considering that my family wasn't the crock-pot kind either.

"Are they going to come here or do I have to go to Inis Mor?" I asked. I shivered when I thought of going to the part of the Other Realm where Slade's parents lived—the Dark side—but I kept my face neutral. I'd never visited the Other Realm at all. While I was intrigued about Slade's homeland, I'd heard stories from Leah about how dangerous and grotesque Dark Créatúir could be when they welcomed visitors.

"You know it isn't safe for you to go to Inis Mor. They'll come here," Slade said slowly. His jaw was still clenched, and he seemed to be sweating like he was uncomfortable. Which I supposed he was, considering that the Créatúir aren't usually all lovey-dovey meet-my-parents.

"Cool. Just let me know when," I said. I glanced across the street and laughed as an old lady clutched her pearl necklace and hurried back into her house. Slade can definitely look scary and intimidating, but he's the last person who would hurt anyone. He just comes off as kind of…ominous. "Creepy" is Leah's term, but ordering a double scoop of vanilla ice cream *with* sprinkles is about as adventurous as she gets.

"Are you coming over right now?" I asked as we walked toward my house.

"Do you need me to?" he said slowly, pointedly.

I shook my head. "I'll be fine." I'd told Slade about the snake and the sand, but downplayed it and hinted that I might've fallen on the banana peel and hit my head. I looked at him with a thin smile. "I'm sure the reptiles will stay away."

He gave me a long look before nodding. "I'll come over later tonight." He quickly kissed the top of my head and then vanished—shifted into air, or something else. It was both a super-cool power and a really annoying one. He could avoid any uncomfortable topics I brought up, like not changing his eye color when he talked to my dad, by shifting away.

I was almost to my street when a newspaper box on the corner caught my eye. On the front of our local paper, just above the big headline about raising the sales tax in town, was this: *CLEOPATRA'S TOMB FOUND?*

My stomach dropped and I started to sweat despite the seventy-degree weather. I quickly dug around in my bag, threw a coin into the machine, and grabbed a paper. I shoved it into my bag and kept walking home, goose bumps and all.

As much as I tried to brush it off, if there was one thing I'd learned in my family, it was this: there are no coincidences. If it makes you pause, if it seems to have meaning, it probably does—and usually in a way that you never expect.

———

I didn't go into the house right away. Instead, I walked around the side and sat down on a flat rock next to my mom's vegetable garden, the only space not taken up by Leah. With my three sisters and psychic mom, there was very little privacy inside; I couldn't focus on the newspaper article while being constantly annoyed.

My hands shaking, I pulled the newspaper out and flipped to the Cleopatra article. Most of it covered the same stuff as the news report: how people had been looking for Cleopatra's tomb for years, and that the archaeologist Paul Coburn thought it was located in the Taposiris Magna region near the Egyptian city of Alexandria. Over time, many historical sites had slid into the Mediterranean due to earthquakes and tidal waves, which was why it was so hard to find the mausoleum. Divers had uncovered statues, monuments, and pieces of important temples, but never Cleopatra's tomb and the treasures that must be contained within it. There was also a map of what Alexandria looked like during the height of Cleopatra's reign, and a reprint of a sketch of her by some guy named Plutarch.

And, in the lower right corner of the page, was a picture of a scroll—which was apparently called a Book of the

Dead. According to the article, people in ancient Egypt were buried with them, and they were considered a gateway or guidebook to the afterlife. The Book had spells for defeating afterlife obstacles and for communicating with people who had already passed on; it seemed like a really creepy version of the handbook I was given when I enrolled at Westerville High. Finding Cleopatra's Book of the Dead, according to Paul Coburn, would be finding "one of the most historically significant artifacts of ancient history."

My mouth felt dry as I squinted at the photo of the Book of the Dead. I didn't know if it was a trick of my eyes or the sunlight or something, but the scroll seemed to shimmer and move on the page like it wanted to float off the paper. I closed my eyes tight and took a deep breath, but a rushing feeling ran up my body, like a swarm of ants eating me.

And then, I was her again.

When I opened my eyes, I was wearing a white robe with a gold belt around the waist. My arms were heavy with gold bracelets, and gold and pearl rings were on every finger. My hands were hennaed and dusted with gold flecks. On my feet were jeweled sandals with carvings of snakes.

I suddenly realized I was moving, and looked around. I was on a floating, flat boat—like a barge made from wood. It seemed to glide along the sparkling water. I was sitting on a gold and red throne, perched high on the back of the barge. Below me sat several ladies-in-waiting, waving feathered fans as servants scurried around like mice, fetching pitchers of water and plates of dates. A few men also sat below, sipping what looked like sweet wine out of jeweled cups. Dozens of muscled, dark men rowed the barge with golden oars.

The air was hot, oppressive, and I was barely able to lift my glittering arm to wave at the crowds of people who gathered on the river banks, waving and shouting at me. Some of the women clutched their children and shouted joyfully. The men beamed at me like I was a prized jewel, and the children stood with their mouths open as though seeing a mirage.

"Beautiful," a voice next to me murmured. He didn't speak in English, but I could understand him. I looked over. He was dressed in a long white robe that matched mine, and wore a crown of leaves. His approving gaze told me that he was in love with me. There was a golden breastplate over his robe. Some part of my brain that actually retained historical facts whispered, *Julius Caesar?*

I studied his face, and my heart stopped when I saw his eyes. They were blue-black, and seemed to be able to change color. Like Slade's.

The breeze picked up and the brilliantly colored flags flapped behind us, snapping in the wind. The crowd began to chant. At first, I couldn't understand what they said because it sounded like a low hum. Then the wind settled down and the flags became silent, and I heard what they were chanting: *Goddess Queen.*

And then I woke up, to Morgana standing over me, her eyes wide.

"What the . . . " I said as I struggled to sit up. I was in my bedroom.

"Oh, thank the realms!" Morgana said as she clasped her hands together. She was dressed very witchlike in a long purple dress with a black rope belt. Her long hair was pulled back from her face and I saw *lexicon* written on her neck—her word of the day, which she calls her "totem."

All that was missing was a house dropped on her and Dorothy with Toto.

"What happened?" I asked as I rubbed my face.

"I found you outside, slumped against the house. I couldn't wake you up so I dragged you into your room before anyone else saw you," Morgana explained. She held up the newspaper article, crumpled and torn. "You were reading this." She tapped the paper for emphasis.

"Oh." I looked away quickly. "I was really tired. I needed to nap." My voice came out all high and squeaky.

Morgana gave me a long look, and I squirmed. I tried to avoid eye contact, but I could feel her gaze boring into my head like a jackhammer. I sighed. "Okay, fine. I've been having a few visions about being Cleopatra." I told her about the snake and the barge. I'd planned on not making it sound like too big a deal, but I wound up throwing my hands in the air as I described the snake and its fangs.

Morgana's expression didn't change as she listened

intently. Finally, when I was done, she said, "We need to call a family meeting and discuss this."

I shook my head. "No way." I wasn't at all prepared to be the subject of a "family discussion." Leah had told my mom about my strange reaction to hearing about the tomb on the news, but I'd been able to downplay the significance of it. If I kept mulling over what was going on, I'd have control over the next move. If I told everyone everything, my mom would go crazy and talk to her spirit guides, and then I'd be stuck doing whatever they decided.

My mom may be psychic, but doesn't always know everything that's going on. Thankfully, she can't predict everything or else I wouldn't have any social life. Her gift is more like a Magic 8 ball—vague and occasionally muddled.

"I just need a little more time to figure out what's going on," I told Morgana.

"Okay, if that's how you want to play this for now. But you have to talk to everyone soon," Morgana said. I nodded silently and waited for her to leave.

My oldest sister stood up and sighed. She reached for the bedroom door, but then stopped and turned around. "When did you start wearing ribbons?" she asked.

"What? I don't." I slowly reached up into my hair and felt a cloth band tied around my head, just behind my ears. I pulled it off and stared at it. I recognized it from the pictures of Cleopatra I'd seen in books and newspapers—it was something called a diadem, and worn by Egyptian royalty since the time of Alexander the Great.

My blood ran cold as I crumpled it into my palm.

THREE

The next Friday night, I tried to push all thoughts of Cleopatra out of my head as I worked the dunk tank at our town's annual fundraiser. The Westerville Festival is a community event with games, food booths, and live music. Since it raises money for the police department, and my dad is on the force, my sisters and I were roped into volunteering.

"You only gave me two tickets," I said from my spot in the booth, staring down the middle-aged guy with glasses who apparently had a serious fondness for the dunk tank. I held my hand out in front of me and tapped my foot.

"No I didn't," he said nervously, glancing around and wringing his hands together.

I looked down at the two red tickets. "Yes. You did. Give me one more or else get out of line."

"Never mind," he said, snatching the tickets out of my hand and scurrying off into the crowd.

"See ya again in about five minutes," I muttered under my breath. I pulled my hair off my neck and fanned my face. It was another warm night, the humidity hanging in the air like a fog that wouldn't go away. It was only June, but we were roasting like pigs on a spit.

"This is ridiculous. What time is it?" I moaned as I leaned forward and put my head in my hands.

"One more hour to go," my little sister Gia said cheerfully.

"Sixty long minutes," I grumbled. My dad had signed us up for the dunk tank because he thought it would be fun, but I'd just spent the last hour handing foam balls to the middle-aged guy who kept trying to scam us out of tickets. He had really, really terrible aim as well.

"Stop being dramatic, Rhea," Morgana said as she surveyed the crowd. A small smile formed on her face as she saw the fortune-teller booth. The fortune-teller was dressed in long white and blue robes and wore a purple turban with a crystal in the center. She waved her long red fingernails above a crystal ball that was clearly made out of plastic. Regardless, there was a long line of impatient festival-goers waiting to hear her wisdom.

"We should go over there and freak that lady out with some of our party tricks," I said.

"Oh yeah? What would your trick be? Sarcastic comments and dramatic flounces?" Leah asked.

I tried to muster up a response, but the humidity killed my desire to argue. I simply gave her a dirty look and pressed my mouth into a thin line.

Truth was, Leah was right. I didn't have any party tricks …and the strange things that were happening to me occurred while I was alone. And I had no answers about what was happening, anyway. After school each night, in between studying for my upcoming finals, I read everything about the Egyptians and reincarnation that I could find, but nothing actually explained why I was having visions. I did read about an Egyptian collection at a museum two hours away. Morgana had agreed to take me there the following weekend, which was also the official start of my summer break.

"Having fun, girls?" my dad asked as he walked up to the booth. He was in uniform, which always makes him look way more important and handsome than when he's just at home, relaxing on the couch. He put his large hands down on the booth's counter and eyed us critically, his large frame bending in half.

"Yep," Gia said. She sighed and leaned against the dunk tank, water sloshing around her feet.

"Good, good. Keep up the hard work and don't slack off." For some reason, Dad stared at me the longest before he walked away.

"I'm exhausted. I was up all night working on a Créatúir funeral," Leah muttered.

I crossed my arms over my chest. "*You're* exhausted?" I

glanced at Morgana. "Doppler kept me up all night howling for food. I swear that cat is like a competitive eater." Doppler is quite possibly the worst-behaved pet in the world, ripping up clothes, peeing in closets, and loving to sleep on my pillow all day so each night I have to lint-roll it before I can lie down. Yet Morgana is convinced that Doppler can predict the weather and is her "spirit animal" or something. I once asked her if it would be possible to adopt a spirit animal who actually used a litter box, but she didn't seem happy about that request.

"He was right about the weather tonight," Morgana said as she pointed to the clear sky.

"For once," I said under my breath. I looked at my watch again and saw that only five minutes had passed. *These are the longest two hours of my life.* Even the policeman sitting in the dunk tank looked like he was going to die of boredom.

At one end of the fairground, a band was playing a terrible cover of "Sweet Home Alabama" while a bunch of adults swayed and spilled drinks on each other. In the middle, food vendors hawked cotton candy, corn dogs, and fried candy bars. We were at the other end, in Game Alley, squished in between the milk-jug ring-toss and the water-cannon race.

I surveyed the crowd, searching for someone I knew. Most of my friends were headed to a party at my friend Ali's house, where I was also going as soon as I could get out of festival jail. I figured all things Egyptian could wait until next weekend when Morgana and I went to the museum.

Across the lawn, I spotted my friends Harper and Reagan and waved them over. "Hey! What are you guys doing here?" I asked. They each held a corn dog in one hand and a cell phone in the other.

Harper shrugged, her long pink extensions waving in the wind. "Just wanted to do a lap before we head to Ali's end-of-the-year party. You're going, right?"

I nodded quickly and glanced at my sisters. "Of course." I was finally off grounding, and I intended to enjoy my freedom before I was inevitably punished for something else.

Reagan waved her corn dog around in the air. "Well, I'm sure everyone is waiting for you."

I laughed. "Right." Truth was, I'd quickly become fairly popular at Westerville. I wasn't one of those Homecoming Queen type of girls, but I didn't have any problems making friends. I guess I just didn't care about other people's "rules," which seemed to both fascinate and shock everyone there. For some reason, being different and standing out has always benefitted me.

"Well, we'll see you later," Harper said, and they turned to leave. As they moved away from my booth, I saw a cute guy with brown hair and a fitted white shirt standing in front of me. He looked a little older than me, maybe closer to eighteen, like Morgana.

"Three tickets," I said and held my hand out.

He studied me for a moment, silent. My hand wavered

in front of him as my stomach dropped a little. His intense gaze made me squirm. "Three tickets," I said again.

He stepped forward and cocked his head to the side, like a cat studying a caged mouse. His eyes were a deep blue, and I could see that he had a tattoo of an eye, behind his ear just under his hairline. What looked like tears fell from the eye, in a lightning-bolt pattern.

He whispered something under his breath, then turned and walked away.

"Hey!" I shouted after him, but he kept walking. I wanted to run after him, but the crowd seemed to swallow him whole, like a snake gulping down a mouse.

"Did you see that strange guy?" I turned to my sisters, but they were all busy fiddling with the plug on the dunk tank, which kept jiggling loose from the outlet.

"What?" Morgana said distractedly.

"Nothing," I said quickly. I scanned the crowd again but didn't see any signs of him.

Normally, I would've just written it off as some escaped prisoner or a druggie, but it was what he'd whispered that I couldn't forget. It was in another language—one that I'd never heard before, except in my dream—but I understood it.

He'd said: "The queen lives again."

Ali's party was in full swing by the time I got Morgana to drop me off across town. As she turned down Ali's street, she whistled low under her breath and I tensed up. Cars lined the road and a bunch were parked all over the lawn. I could hear the music even from inside our car, and for a moment I hesitated.

"This looks pretty risky, Rhea," Morgana said as she squinted through the windshield at a group of freshmen heading toward the house. *First high school party*, I thought as I watched them nervously flick their long straight hair.

I waved my hand dismissively. "It's fine. I won't stay long. Slade's meeting me here and driving me home later anyway." Despite my confident words, I swallowed quickly and swore I'd just pop in and out. I really, really didn't want to be grounded. Again.

A look flashed across Morgana's eyes and I could practically hear her thinking, O*h, good. Slade. That's not much better than some wild party.*

Even though Slade had worked with Leah in that nasty Créatúir war, my family wasn't a particularly huge fan of his. I suppose it was either because he was (a) not human, (b) a Dark Créatúir—not a fluffy Light Créatúir, and (c) occasionally looked like he belonged in a biker bar. But it didn't matter—he was a great guy and my sisters weren't the ones dating him. Besides, he just *looked* ominous. I felt like they of all people shouldn't judge someone, or something, by appearances.

"Thanks for the ride," I said quickly, and wrenched the door open before Morgana could start an interrogation. I glanced nervously at the house, which seemed to shake down to its foundation from the music.

I won't stay long, I repeated to myself silently.

"Rhea!" Ali screeched as I opened the front door. She threw her arms around me and hugged me. "So glad you're here! How was the festival?"

"As exciting as you can imagine."

Ali's friends started to gather around me, saying things like, "Awesome shoes! Love your hair! Super cute nail polish." I nodded thanks and started backing away, toward the kitchen where I heard Harper and Reagan.

"You're here!" Harper waved at me from behind the island.

"Barely," I said. "This party is insane. It's like a sardine can in here."

"Want a drink?" asked Mark Masterson, Homecoming King and all-around Mr. High School. I shook my head and he stepped toward me. "Want anything else?"

I held up my palm. "No way. And back off. You're becoming stalker levels of creepy." Mark had been trying to hook up with me since I started at Westerville. Needless to say, his batting average with me was 0.0, and was going to stay that way.

"Look who joined the party!" Chris Burke shouted from the doorway. He appeared with a huge brown and white boa constrictor around his neck. I'd heard he sometimes brought "Judy" to parties with him, but I always assumed it was like a metaphor or an urban legend.

"Eek!" Reagan shrieked as she shrank away from Chris. He responded by waggling the boa constrictor's head in her face.

I stepped back farther and pressed against the countertop, which cut into my skin. I hated snakes. No, "hated" isn't a strong enough word. Whatever comes after hatred—that's how I felt about snakes. It wasn't just because of the creepy vision, either; I'd always felt this way. A leftover from my previous life—literally. Some things don't go away even after two thousand years.

"It's way too crowded in here," I said quickly. I shoved a bunch of people aside and wrenched open the front door.

"Rhea! Don't leave! Let's toast to having the greatest summer of our lives!" I heard Ali say. I sighed. It's not that I didn't like having friends, but it got exhausting to keep up with everyone. It always seemed like people wanted a piece of me wherever I went.

I could hear Reagan and Harper inside calling my name, so I stepped into a dark part of the porch to hide before I glanced inside.

And then I saw him. The guy with the tattoo, from the festival, who'd whispered something I couldn't really hear… but which told me he knew my secret. He was standing inside by himself, obviously searching for someone.

A chill ran down my spine as I wondered if that some-one was me.

Stop being insane. He's probably from another school and searching for his friends. Or his lost dog.

Regardless, I didn't want to stick around to find out. I flipped open my phone to call Slade and escape the party before it got busted. But I was distracted by a scuffle on the lawn. Turning, I saw Troy, king of all things jock, star-ing down little Steve Withers.

"Dude, I said get the hell out of here! This party isn't for rejects!" Troy said, clearly drunk, spitting his words all over Steve.

Steve shrank back at Troy's humongous size and quickly moved away. I couldn't help myself, so I stepped off the porch and jogged over to them.

"Not for rejects? Then what are you doing here, Troy?" I asked, hands on my hips. Troy was such a nightmare: fat, drunk, gross, sweaty, and with a sense of entitlement just because he was on the football team.

"Funny, Rhea," Troy slurred. He stepped toward me. "How about you and I go inside and get a drink together?"

"Dream on, loser." I rolled my eyes and shot a look at Steve, who responded with a grateful smile. "In fact, I think you should—" I didn't get to finish my sentence, thanks to the sudden whirl of blue and white police lights in front of the house.

"COPS!" everyone seemed to shout at once, before trying to scatter in the wind.

I started to turn, to run down the block, when I heard "Rhea! Rhea Spencer! Stop right there!"

Oh crap.

I turned and squinted into the darkness. It was Jim Albert, the policeman who'd been stuck in the dunk tank. I sighed and shook my head.

Busted.

A few minutes later, I was sitting in the back of the cop car, watching my friends give the cops fake names. I again wished I had some cool power. I could turn the cop car into a pumpkin or shapeshift into a lightning bug or put a spell on everyone that would make them forget my name.

Something. Anything.

But no, I was stuck with this lame, slowly-getting-weirder power of…nothing.

I sighed and put my head in my hands.

My dad was officially going to kill me. For real this time.

FOUR

Y ou're kinda cute." The dirty, shaky guy across the holding cell leered at me like a stray dog drooling over a bone.

"Go away. Stop talking to me," I said, mustering up as dirty a look as I could. It wasn't easy, since I'd been crying for the past two hours. The shaky guy had been in there with me for only ten minutes, but he hadn't stopped alternately talking to himself about mashed potatoes and staring at me.

If my father wanted to punish me, he was certainly going all out.

I wasn't technically "arrested," but—lucky me—thanks to my dad's position on the squad, they made a special exception and threw me into a holding cell as some kind of Scared Straight thing. I wasn't screamed at by convicted felons, but I did have to deal with my cellmate, who clearly was going through some kind of narcotics withdrawal.

Officer Albert had dropped me off in the cell without a word. Whenever I asked where my dad was, the cops just said, "Oh, you'll see him later." When I asked them if I could get my one phone call, like I saw in the movies, they laughed and shook their heads. "I have rights, you know!" I shrieked, like I'd seen on an episode of *Law and Order*, but they didn't seem to care. Suddenly, Westerville seemed more like Guantanamo Bay than a nice small town obsessed with high school football.

I sank down on the cold cement bench, pressing my elbows into my sides and trying to ignore my cellmate. Just as I was about to start whistling "Back on the Chain Gang," I spotted a German Shepherd in the office area. He was huge, much bigger than any Shepherd I'd ever seen. And he was staring right at me with brilliant amber eyes.

The policeman holding the leash wasn't paying attention—he was actually, stereotypically, eating a donut and drinking coffee. The dog waited for the policeman to let the leash go slack, then casually walked over to my cell. It shimmered for a moment, then shifted into a spider on the floor, crawled into my cell, and then shifted into Slade— hidden in the corner's shadow, out of sight.

My cellmate let out a low whistle and clapped his hands together. I'm sure he'd seen something like that before, albeit a hallucination.

"Quiet." Slade held up his hand and silenced the guy. He always had that effect on people—they generally were too freaked out to disobey him. He walked over to me and placed a hand on my cheek. "What happened?"

My face crumpled for a moment before I took a long, slow breath. "Wrong place, wrong time. I was only at the party for like five minutes before they busted it. My parents are going to kill—" This time, I couldn't stop the tears.

Slade put his hands on my shoulders and pulled me toward his long frame. He wasn't usually one for big displays of emotion, but he held me tight as I cried. I was trying to remain quiet, since the last thing I needed was any policemen thinking I'd smuggled my not-quite-human boyfriend into jail with me.

"And there's—something else," I said in between muffled sobs.

"What?" he said into my hair.

I pulled away from him and looked up into his eyes, which were violet now. "I'm having dreams … visions … something. Where I'm Cleopatra, but it's almost like they're memories. And twice tonight I've seen this strange guy with a tattoo. He said something to me, too, but I didn't understand why." I shook my head and brushed my hair out of my eyes.

Slade grasped my shoulders firmly. "Nothing will happen to you. I will watch over you. And I will find out who this guy is."

I smiled thinly. "Thanks, but I can watch over myself. I'm not really the damsel-in-distress type, you know that."

He smiled, something he rarely did with anyone other than me. He mostly frowned at Leah, a fact I kind of relished. "I know. But this is serious. This guy could be dangerous."

"I—" Suddenly, Slade shifted back outside the cell and I was standing by myself. "Sla—" I started to say, when I heard another voice.

"Rhea Spencer."

My mother. Crap.

"Do you know how much pain you've caused?" Mom stood in front of me, lines creasing her tanned forehead. She shook her head, her curly hair brushing against the river-rock earrings she found in Sedona.

"Mom, I—" I tried to say, but she cut me off. *Uh oh. Interrupting. Not good.*

"Stop. You listen, and I talk. Morpheus has been telling me for days that something is off with you. I just didn't want to believe it."

I rolled my eyes. Morpheus. He's my mom's main spirit guide and never fails to tattle on me. He seems to be less of a spiritual guide and more of a fun-ruiner. One time, I got in trouble just because I *thought* about taking the car out without my learner's permit.

"Don't you roll your eyes at me!" Mom snapped. Policemen in the precinct were starting to stare at us, and even my cellmate slunk back. My mom is generally peaceful, but can be terrifying when upset.

I sighed and faced her, trying to put on my most contrite look since I wasn't at all ready to involve the whole family in what might or might not be happening to me. Slade and Morgana were enough of a support team for now. "I'm sorry, Mom. It was a stupid mistake. It won't happen again, and everything is fine with me, really. Morpheus is just being weird."

My mom gave me a long look, clearly not believing anything I'd just said. But she knew better than to keep pushing. "Well, you're grounded until at least the next full moon."

"Wonderful," I muttered. The previous night had been a full moon, so that meant a whole month at home, with my sisters to torture me. Sixteen was definitely shaping up to be my worst year yet.

My mom motioned for the guard to open the cell, and I followed her out. "Don't forget, it's your turn to polish the crystals tonight," she said.

Before we left, I glanced back at my cellmate, whose mouth was hanging open. The last thing I heard before we left the precinct was him call out, "Are you guys wizards?"

FIVE

I once read that prisoners in jail get at least one hour of outside exercise and free time each day. After being grounded for a week, I decided that any maximum-security facility was preferable to the Spencer Penitentiary, especially right before summer break. The previous seven days had been one long mush of hours, thanks to finals, interrupted only by an escort home from school each afternoon by Leah and Ben. I had to listen to their boring conversation about whether spicy or regular yellow mustard was better, and I didn't even have Slade around to laugh about it with afterward. Of course, since he's a shapeshifter he could've easily gotten around the whole physical barrier—morphing into a tree branch and then hopping into my room—but my mom was watching me so closely, I knew she'd figure it out. Not to mention that Warden Morpheus wouldn't hesitate to tattle. Funny thing was, I think my mom was more upset than my dad about everything. It was like he was secretly a little pleased that one of his daughters had gone out and done something so "normal."

So, I sat at home every night and watched television with Gia as I pretended to study for finals. It was enough to make me go crazier than I already was.

I didn't have any more visions, but that last one, triggered by the photo of the Book of the Dead, was never far from my mind. Thankfully, when the weekend came, Morgana and I headed to the Natural History Museum, two hours away in Beachfield.

After Morgana parked the car, we made our way up concrete steps flanked by gold lions. The museum had just opened, but there was already a line to buy tickets. I swayed back and forth, exhaling loudly, until finally we paid and were inside.

"Should we head straight to the Ancient Egypt exhibit?" Morgana asked, squinting at a crumpled museum floor plan.

"Let's do it," I said firmly. My heart started to race as I followed my sister toward the elevators. I'd read online that this museum had a lot of artifacts from Ancient Egypt and that the curator specialized in Egyptology. I wasn't sure exactly what we were looking for, but I thought that seeing the artifacts—and, in a way, letting *them* see *me*—might give me a few clues about what had started on my sixteenth birthday.

We stepped off the elevator and I followed my sister through the winding hallways, seeing arrowheads from caveman times and pottery from China, and a bunch of taxidermied animals that were both creepy and sad. After a while, it felt like almost anything from the past could be put in this museum as culturally significant. Then, finally, we entered the Ancient Egypt area.

"Ready?" Morgana raised her eyebrows and smiled.

"Mmm hmmm." I walked toward a stone tablet carved with hieroglyphs, my pulse pounding despite my neutral face.

"Are you all right?" she asked, but I ignored her.

I stared up at the intricately carved tablet. It was carved with a pattern that repeated: an eye, a long staff, and some spiral squiggles. I waited for something to happen, to suddenly be able to read the tablet, but it stayed silent.

"Hmmmm," I said. I walked over to a replica of a sarcophagus. It stood tall in front of me, gold and amber inlays in the casket covering the mummy. I shivered as I read the description of how people were mummified—their brains pulled out their noses by a long, silver hook.

Was that what happened to me … to her?

"Look at this," Morgana said. I walked over and stood in front of a crumbling brown scroll. There were colorful drawings of pyramids, strange birds with human eyes, and people with the heads of dogs. Cursive hieroglyphs were written in long, vertical lines.

"It says here that this is a Book of the Dead," Morgana

said. "When someone died, they were buried with it, and it was supposed to be their guide to the Underworld."

"Mmm hmmm." I'd learned that from the newspaper article about Cleopatra.

On one part of the scroll was an illustration of a dog-like priest of some sort, with a head like a jackal. He wore a long blue headdress and held up a scale with a human heart on one side, a feather on the other. I read the description:

In the Hall of Ma'at, the deceased's heart, the location of his soul, was weighed against the Feather of Truth. If the heart was pure, it would be lighter than the feather and the person was granted entrance to the Underworld.

My eyes widened and a chill ran through me at the idea of weighing a human heart.

I saw a shadow out of the corner of my eye. *Slade?*

But it wasn't him at all.

A figure stepped out of the shadows. It was the same guy from the festival and Ali's party. I whipped my head back around and tried to read the information about the Book again.

"Wow, this is so interesting. It was their version of a spell book. How cool," Morgana said as she tapped the placard.

The guy stepped next to me, nearly touching my shoulder. My scalp began to sweat and I pressed my hands together in front of me. And then he spoke.

"You are in danger," he said. His voice was deep and soft.

I cleared my throat loudly, but didn't turn my head toward him. "Yeah, from you, stalker. Who are you?" I asked.

"They're coming for you. And they will find you," he said.

I was about to turn toward him, to shove him against the wall and ask what the heck was going on, but then— the Book. It started to move. All the symbols and words and drawings began to dance together, shimmering in the case. The dog-priest with human eyes floated above the scroll, looked at me, and barked. It nodded its head as if acknowledging royalty.

I rubbed my eyes, and the images returned to the Book where they belonged. And, of course, the guy was gone.

"Did you see that man? Where did he go?" I said quickly, grabbing Morgana's arm.

"I don't know." She craned her neck and looked around the crowd. "Did you hear his voice?" she continued. "He was speaking in another language, but I couldn't place which one. It sounded like something from another world." She glanced back at the Book, and her eyes scanned the display case. She pushed a button and a voice came out, in another language. "Like this!"

I listened to the recording, and realized he must have been speaking in ancient Egyptian.

And I'd understood all of it.

Morgana touched my arm. "Are you all right?"

I shook my head. "I need to find out who that guy is...and what he knows about me."

———————

In my dream that night, I sat on an intricate throne of gold and pearl with gold bangles stacked up my arms. On my finger was a giant amber ring, large enough to make it difficult to lift my hand. Seated around me were ladies-in-waiting, dressed in more muted versions of my attire. My hair was wound into a braid at the back of my head, and when I gingerly reached back and touched it, I could feel small round pearls woven through it.

The ceiling above me soared high, and beautiful artwork of the pyramids and the eye of Ra watched over the great hall. I sat on the throne alone, but beneath me were groups of male courtiers seated at long tables, waiting to receive palace guests.

"The scribe Aquinias," whispered one of the courtesans. I noticed a small, sprightly man staring at me.

"Your Majesty," said the scribe. He bowed, and I noticed that he wore a white robe and sandals. I motioned for him to come closer and he approached my throne, his robe swishing against the stairs. "I come bearing the precious gift Your Majesty asked me to make." He extended his arms forward, head bowed, and made his offering.

In his arms was a scroll. It looked similar to the Book of the Dead scroll I'd seen in the museum, but it was bigger, and longer, and decorated with gold swirls on the edges. As I reached out and took it, its heaviness surprised me. I carefully ran a finger along the delicate gold-leaf hieroglyphs, then slowly unrolled it and glanced at the inside, electricity running through my fingers as I touched it.

My hands trembled as I scanned the pictures of horrible beasts, of half-man/half-demons guarding the entrance to the underworld and the afterlife. The text was written mostly in black ink, except for a few words in red.

The hieroglyphs on the inside looked like they were in cursive, just like the hieroglyphs on the scroll at the museum. I saw the same illustration, of the priest weighing a human heart against a feather. *This must be a Book of the Dead*, I thought. I remembered the museum placard saying that it was often royalty who commissioned a personal Book of the Dead, since they were very expensive to produce.

"It's beautiful," I whispered to the scribe.

He bowed his head deeply and smiled. "Not more beautiful than Her Majesty, of course." His eyes flicked to the illustration of the heart. "The Book will not fail you. It will guide you through this life and the next."

I nodded and instinctively pulled the scroll toward my chest, guarding it. It belonged to me—I felt it.

"Thank you," I said.

"Do not let it out of your sight," the scribe said with another bow. "It holds great power."

As he turned to leave, I saw—behind his ear—a tattoo

of an eye, with tears running from it in a jagged pattern like a lightning bolt.

The ladies-in-waiting murmured around me and pointed toward the Book, nodding their heads in reverence. I curled my fingers tighter around it, determined to protect it at any cost.

SIX

A flash of lightning smeared across the night sky as a rumble of thunder sounded, muffled in the distance. I peeked through the front-door window and saw a tree branch blow down the street. Another rumble of thunder, and the lights in my house flickered. My heart stopped for a moment, and then I exhaled as the power stayed on. As if it wasn't creepy enough to be stuck home alone during a storm, I didn't need to be sitting in the dark like some horror movie chick waiting to get hacked to pieces, possibly by my Egyptian-speaking stalker.

Morgana and I had searched the museum for him, but he was gone. Again. I'd looked over my shoulder all weekend, but he had apparently decided to keep his distance.

I was still under house arrest due to my run-in with

the law. It was Sunday night, and my parents were out with friends, Leah was doing something with Ben, and Morgana was participating in her weekly drum circle. Even Gia was out with a client. So it was just me and Doppler, who slunk around the house like he was the one being stalked.

"Shouldn't you have been prepared for this, psychic cat?" I muttered in his direction as I got settled in the living room. He responded by making a beeline for my lap.

I flipped on the television, but every channel was painted with red warnings and maps of the storm's path. *Fantastic*, I thought. I turned to a reality show in the hope that other people's life disasters would make mine seem less intense.

I was half-listening to some clueless couple try to work through an obstacle course in the jungle when I heard a long *creeeek* outside on the front porch. Noises in our house were nothing unusual. Considering my mom's profession—considering all our activities, I guess—there always seemed to be some shadow moving or incense burning; in fact, it wasn't strange at all to walk into a room and find my mom or my sisters talking to an invisible entity. But they usually didn't creep around on the front porch like they were trying to break into the house.

I tensed up and listened, my head cocked to the side. Then I heard another noise. It was another long *creeeek* on the porch, but heavier. And then another one. Each one growing closer.

It sounded like footsteps. Heading straight for the front door.

Doppler's ears turned toward the porch and I felt him tense. Then, another *creeek* and he jumped off my lap, digging his claws into my leg on the way down.

"Ow!" I shrieked as I saw the thin scratches start to turn red with blood. I stood up and hobbled toward the kitchen, my thigh burning. The phone was only a few steps away and I knew the police response would be fast, thanks to my dad.

"Slade?" I called thinly into the air. Yet I knew it couldn't be him. He had to attend some all-important, secretive Créatúir meeting in Inis Mor. Time moves much more slowly in his realm, so he was going to be there until at least the next day.

My heart was pounding and my palms were wet as I grabbed the phone. And then, I heard the front door open.

My head snapped around as I tried to figure out if I should hide or run out the back door. Just as I decided to make a run for it, I heard, "Rhea? Don't be scared."

I remained silent, holding my breath as the footsteps approached the kitchen. Who should appear in front of me but the guy from the festival and the museum.

"Get out! My father is a cop and he has a huge gun!" I shrieked as I dropped the phone.

"I'm sorry. I didn't mean to scare you, but I needed to

talk to you." He was wearing dark jeans and a white T-shirt, with muddy black boots that were tracking dirt everywhere on the tile floor. He held his hands up in front of him.

"What do you want?" I backed away and pressed myself against the kitchen counter. Another couple of steps and I could run past him to the front door if he tried anything funky.

"Did you understand what I said in the museum? When I spoke in Egyptian? It was a test. According to the prophecy, the true queen will understand ancient Egyptian."

"So what if I did?" My voice shook but I put my hands on my hips. "Again, who are you and what the hell do you want?"

He looked down at the mud on the floor and smiled sheepishly. "Sorry. Please, let's sit." Wordlessly, I followed him to the kitchen table. "My name is Declan," he continued. "I'm here to warn you that you're in danger."

"Yeah, I got that." I waved my hand around. "You seem to be the dangerous one around here!"

The guy—Declan, apparently—sighed and looked at his hands for a moment. I guess he expected me to fall on the floor, my teeth chattering, and beg for his protection. "Look, we know who you are. We know you're the reincarnation of Cleopatra—of the last queen of Egypt."

I forced my face to remain neutral and made a nondescript sound. "Continue," I said.

He clasped his hands and looked serious, as though he had prepared for this moment. "I'm a member of the Order of Antony, an ancient brotherhood originally formed in the first century BC. We were organized specifically by Mark Antony, and our job is to protect certain secrets—and people." He looked at me, trying to gauge my reaction.

I nodded, but didn't react. I wanted him to realize I wasn't the kind of girl who was going to fall on her knees in shock at a few ancient secrets. "Okay," I said. I slowly bent down and grabbed the phone, still not ready to let my guard down.

His voice wavered in surprise, but he continued. "As you may have heard, a group of archaeologists is closing in on the location of Cleopatra's tomb. There are certain artifacts within it that, if they fall into the wrong hands, will prove dangerous to the world—and you."

I cleared my throat. "Like what?"

Declan impatiently ran a hand through his hair. "Picture end-of-the-world type destruction and the natural order of things going awry."

I swallowed the lump in my throat. "Sounds epic."

Declan slammed his hand down on the table and my mom's waterfall centerpiece jumped and shattered, spilling rocks and water all over the kitchen. I ignored it and focused on Declan. "Don't you get it? These archaeologists aren't just any group of regular archaeologists. They're part of an organization called the Octavians, and they want you. *You*, Rhea. They know that you're the key to unlocking the magic of the treasure within Cleopatra's tomb. You're the only one the artifacts will respond to, so they're going to kidnap you and bring you to the tomb. And then use you for their own purposes."

Now *that* sounded like I should start paying attention.

"What?" I whispered. I definitely did not want to have anything to do with words like "kidnap" and "use you for their own purposes."

"Well, the fact that you're still here, unharmed, means they haven't found you yet. But I'm sure they're close." Declan stood up and extended his hand. "Come with me and we will keep you safe, in hiding."

I started to reach my hand forward and then pulled it back, quickly. *What am I thinking? I can't go into hiding. I don't even know this guy.* I shook my head. "No. I can take care of myself. I have three really gifted sisters, a psychic mom, a policeman dad, and a boyfriend who, let's just say, is extraordinary."

Declan sighed and rubbed his temples. "You don't know what lengths they'll go to get to you. The only way you can be sure of your safety is with us."

I crossed my arms over my chest. "I don't even know you. How do I know *you're* not an Octavian, by the way?"

He turned his head and pointed to the tattoo behind his ear. It was in fact the same tattoo from my dream: an eye with a lightning-bolt tear. "It's the Order's symbol. You must believe that."

I narrowed my eyes and gave him a skeptical look.

He sighed. "If I were an Octavian, wouldn't I just kidnap you right now? Would I even sit here and explain all this?"

It made sense, but I still leaned away from him. "Sure, but why would the Order send you? You're young. If you guys are an ancient, powerful, secret organization, why were *you* appointed to come talk to me?"

"Because I volunteered. And as the youngest member, they thought I could more easily convince you than, say, a sixty-year-old guy." His eyes hinted at a smile.

True. I'd probably just think it was some poor old man from the nursing home who'd lost his way. My mouth twisted around and I nodded.

"So you'll come with me?" he said.

I shook my head. "I'm not totally insane. I'm not just going to leave with some stranger who breaks into my house."

"Really? Because what would you have done if one of the Octavians had walked through that door tonight instead of me?" Declan looked at me intensely, his blue eyes dark.

Another lump formed in my throat as I shrugged and looked away. I knew the answer, though: I would have been in big, big trouble.

"This is a lot of information to digest," I said finally. "I need to think all this through. And maybe you guys could just keep an eye out from a distance," I offered.

Declan gave me a long look. "I know enough about the Great Queen to know that I won't be able to convince you differently. We will keep our distance, as you wish, but just know that we might not be here in time if something happens quickly."

A chill ran down my spine, but I nodded. "Got it." As Declan turned to leave, mud still tracking everywhere, I quickly added, "Oh, and Declan? How did you find me? I mean, how did you find out my secret?"

Declan stopped, and then slowly turned around. The look on his face made the hair on the back of my neck stand up. "An ancient prophecy states that the queen will be reincarnated. On her sixteenth birthday, the Star of Duat will appear closer to the Earth than it has in more than two thousand years—and it will appear above the approximate location of the reincarnated queen. On your birthday, the star appeared above you in the sky. We started looking then, and we were certainly helped by the fact that your family is rumored to be, shall we say, unusual."

I swallowed hard. When he reached for the door, he paused and looked back at me. "The fact that they are about to open the tomb likely means they're already close to finding you. As I mentioned, they'll stop at nothing to acquire you." He gave me a long, hard look. "They've waited over two thousand years for you to be born—remember that."

My stomach clenched, and he disappeared into the night.

I started to wonder just what my sixteenth year had in store.

SEVEN

I woke up early the next day, my mind still trying to sort through what Declan had said. My family had gotten home late, and I didn't have a chance to tell anyone what was going on before I fell asleep. Slade was still in Inis Mor, and Morgana had ended up spending the night at a fellow Wiccan's house.

I walked around the neighborhood, hoping the fresh air would clear my head, while I waited for Morgana to come home. After an hour, I felt ready to tell her what happened. She usually had a logical perspective on strange events and I knew she would ask all the right questions. My brain kept repeating what Declan had said about the Octavians waiting over two thousand years for me to be born, and I couldn't help but see the irony—my own family would barely wait for me to finish getting dressed before leaving the house.

I walked home, trying not to think about the fact that all of this certainly wasn't going to just go away. As I turned down my street, I heard the screech of tires. But before I could look in the direction of the sound, two hands roughly grabbed my upper arms and yanked me backward. I fell onto the sidewalk and my head hit the concrete.

"Stop!" I screamed as the dark figure above me dragged me by the arms onto the grass. I kicked my legs up, connecting with the person, but it was no use. He was stronger—much stronger—than me and I was like a tiny mosquito buzzing around him. I felt another pair of hands grab my ankles, and then I was helpless. It all happened so fast that I didn't have time to mount a plan of escape.

I tried to look up and see who was attacking me, but the sun was in my eyes. I felt a warm sticky liquid drip down my neck and I realized that my head was cut. I saw a white blob parked in the street and thought with horror, "This is it. I'm being kidnapped. They're taking me to that white van."

As they lifted my body to put me into the van, they suddenly stopped. One of them let out a low moan and crumpled to the ground. I hit the street with a hard thud, my arm scraping across the broken glass on the curb. I moaned and curled up as bright red blood trickled down my forearm. There was someone else with us, someone who was hitting my kidnappers. I heard the van doors close and the car screech away.

"Oh no," I whimpered as I looked down at my arm. There was a jagged piece of glass sticking out, and a bright red stream of blood dripped onto the curb.

"What happened?" Slade asked. He sat down on the curb next to me, his amber colored eyes dilating. "Who were those guys?" He put one hand on either side of my face and studied my eyes.

"I—" As I started to speak, everything went black, and I slumped forward against my boyfriend.

EIGHT

Hit him harder," Slade instructed.

I wiped a bead of sweat off my forehead and exhaled, then bent my knees and put my hands up in front of my face in an attack stance. I stared down my opponent and threw a left hook forward. Just as I was about to connect with his face, he shifted into a wolf and then back to his Créatúir form, so I wound up swinging in the air, my body flailing around. He threw a leg out and swept my feet out from under me, and I landed hard on my back. I gasped for breath as I rolled around.

"Get up," my opponent said with a laugh.

I rolled onto my side and gingerly stood up. "Not fair!" I screeched as I clutched my bandaged arm to my body. Slade put his arms on my shoulders to steady me, and my opponent threw his head back and laughed again, his long tongue forking and then closing up.

"You have to be prepared for anything. How do you know these people don't have any magical abilities?" Slade asked.

"This is ridiculous," I snapped at him. After the near-kidnapping, Slade had insisted that I learn to defend myself. Except instead of being a normal boyfriend, who would find his normal girlfriend a nice self-defense class at the YMCA, Slade hired Asher, his Créatúir buddy, who was trained in magical martial arts. We were working in an indoor gym that Slade had rented out for the afternoon. So far, Asher had disappeared, shapeshifted, and nearly torched me breathing fire. At this rate, I was going to return home in worse shape than after the attempted kidnapping.

Already, my summer vacation was turning out to be less than ideal.

I adjusted the wrap on my wrist and gingerly touched the butterfly bandage over my eyebrow. After Slade had scared my would-be kidnappers away, he tried to take me to the hospital, but I refused. I really didn't want to try and explain to a doctor what had happened. So Slade took me to Leah, who called the Créatúir Nuala to help heal my wounds. Except she kind of got distracted in the middle due to some rumblings in the Other Realm, and I was left to do half the healing the old-fashioned way.

Leah didn't ask many questions, but the rest of my family did. I was vague giving out information—I told them I'd tripped on the sidewalk—except with Morgana. I let her in on what Declan had told me, and she agreed that being trained in self-defense was a good move for now, while we figured out our next move. She did some research on the star of Duat, the Book of the Dead, Mark Antony, and Octavian and said they all seemed to check out.

"Again," Slade said.

I started to crouch down, then shook my head. "Enough. I'm exhausted." I waved my bandaged arm around, the one the glass lacerated and nearly amputated. "I'm injured, remember?"

Slade nodded and waved Asher off. Asher backed against the wall and eyed me suspiciously. "She's so weak," he muttered. His forked tongue licked the outside of his lips.

"I heard that, jerk," I retorted.

"You were supposed to," he said. His pupils dilated as he looked me up and down. "You're lucky Slade is so influential in our world or else I wouldn't be wasting my time here. I'd probably just kill you now and get it over with."

"Er, thanks?" I said sarcastically. "The feeling is mutual. Spending time with you is not exactly a treat." I bent down and started to shove my sweatshirt into my bag, eager to get away from Asher.

"And about to get a lot more influential," Asher muttered to himself.

"Asher," Slade said in a warning tone. He stepped away from the wall and stood in front of Asher, who shrank back a little.

"What? What is he talking about?" I snapped my head between the two of them . . . Slade never used that tone unless something was important.

"You haven't told her yet?" Asher asked. He shook his head and looked away before disappearing, leaving a wisp of smoke that dissipated quickly.

Slade sighed loudly.

"I'm waiting," I said. I walked over to him and stood in front of him, hands on my hips. "Well?"

Slade glanced outside, at Declan loitering on the sidewalk. After hearing about the attack on me, Declan became very obvious following me around—a fact that Slade was not too thrilled about.

"Forget about him." I waved my hand dismissively in Declan's direction. I stood in front of the window and blocked Slade's view. "What's going on?"

Slade gave me a long look, his amber eyes soft, and my heart jumped into my chest. "The day you were attacked?" he said. I nodded. "The High Council told me they want me to be the King of the Dark Créatúir when Queen Kiera steps down next season."

I heard what he said, but my ears buzzed and I presumed I had gone deaf for moment. He couldn't have said what I thought he did. "What?"

"They want me to be king," he said quietly.

"I heard you. I'm just—just surprised." Slade being King of the Dark Créatúir would mean so many things—one of which was that he would likely have to stay in the Other Realm. Permanently. "Wow. That's so great." My voice was hollow and my hands started to shake.

So this was it. I always knew that things were a little hazy with Slade when it came to the whole being-together-forever thing, but I didn't expect it to end so soon. While my life often operated without a concrete plan, it usually worked out and I'd assumed this would be no different.

"Rhea," he started, reaching for my hand, but I pulled away and crossed my arms over my chest. I couldn't let him touch me; it would make the whole situation worse.

"Does Leah know?" I asked.

Slade looked away, and I knew she did.

"I'm going to kill her!" I shrieked. "How could she keep this from me?"

Slade took a step toward me and put his hand on my cheek. I closed my eyes and tears threatened to spill down my cheeks.

"Everything okay in here?" Declan asked from the doorway. Slade quickly pulled his hand back. "I thought I heard yelling."

"I'm fine," I said quickly. I wrapped my sweatshirt around my waist and hugged my arms to my chest again.

Declan gave me a long look and then glanced at Slade. "Are you going to take her home?"

"I'm going by myself. I need to be alone," I said, and stormed toward the door. I knew it probably wasn't the smartest idea in the world after my near-kidnapping, but I just needed a few minutes to clear my head. I figured I could walk quickly and keep my eyes open.

Declan caught my bag and stopped me short. "That's not safe," he said. I tried to wrench my bag away from him but he held onto it. "They're watching you."

"Yeah, yeah," I muttered, rolling my eyes.

"Rhea, the Octavians have the Book. They pulled it out of the tomb this morning. I'm sure that's why they tried to grab you the other day." Declan's eyes were dark.

I shook my head, my thoughts crashing together.

"You have to tell your family what's going on—all of them," Declan said.

I waited for Slade to protest, but he nodded in agreement.

"Wonderful," I said. *So now I think my boyfriend just broke up with me and I have to tell my parents that Octavians are after me.*

And I thought being grounded was painful.

———

My family was gathered in the kitchen, prepping dinner, when Slade and I walked through the front door. Declan wanted to come in with us, but I waved him off. Knowing my sisters, they would fawn all over him and get the wrong idea. Besides, I was sure my family would be level-headed about the situation and trust my judgment, and then I could tell Declan to back off a little.

"Are you okay?" Slade asked.

I nodded but remained silent. My brain was still trying to process what he'd told me about being asked to become king. I had so many questions for him, but I had to deal with this situation first.

"Everyone, I have an announcement," I said. My family froze where they were—my mom stopped stirring the spaghetti sauce, Leah paused with a fork in her hand while setting the table, Gia stopped in mid-pour of lemonade, and Morgana stopped blessing the food. Only my dad continued tossing a salad. I shot Leah a dirty look and she pretended not to notice.

"Oh great," my dad grumbled, and he sat down. He looked at Slade and his eyes narrowed.

I glanced at my mom, whose face was neutral. Figures. She probably already knew. I leaned in Slade's direction a little and took a deep breath. "Okay, so I'm going to say this quickly and then we can eat." I nervously played with the bag on my hip. I quickly told them about the visions and my visit from Declan. I left out the part about Declan wanting me to hide out with the Order.

No one spoke, so I took a step forward. "Spaghetti? Yum." I turned to Slade. "I need to talk to you before you leave."

"What the hell are you talking about?" My dad spoke first. He was still wearing his police officer uniform, and he leaned forward and placed his forehead in his hands.

"Like I said, I've got it covered." I sat down at the table and started to reach for the garlic bread. I figured if I just threw the information out there and then diverted their attention, this all would go away. Like when I enticed the cat to leave my sweaters alone by throwing catnip on the kitchen floor.

"I can't believe you don't think this is a big deal." Leah's hands were on her hips and she shot Slade an accusing look.

"It *is* a big deal. It's how she got those injuries," Slade said quietly. "The Octavians tried to grab her a few days ago and I scared them away."

My mom walked over to me and hugged my head against her. "I was afraid something like this would happen to you. I knew you were in danger, but I didn't know how or when or from whom."

"Like I said, what the hell is going on?" my dad said.

My mom held her hand up, her eyes closed. "This is real. I can feel it. She's in danger." She turned to Morgana. "So, you knew about this? Why didn't you tell me?"

Morgana shook her head. "I'm sorry. I was trying to do

what was best. I thought she would be safe, but…" Her voice trailed off as she glanced at my arm.

There was a loud bang as my dad slammed his hand on the table. "Safe, my foot!"

"Maybe some guys from the force could protect me?" I offered, my voice high and squeaky. Hiding was definitely not my thing. At all.

"Yeah, that sounds reasonable." Leah exhaled loudly and rolled her eyes.

Slade cleared his throat and shook his head. "Declan wants her to stay with the Order."

"You're going to, aren't you?" Gia said, her eyes wide.

Damn.

"I don't even know if they're legit. I—"

Morgana interrupted me. "I've researched everything. It seems to add up. You should probably go stay with them." She gave me a sympathetic look. "I'm sorry. I know that's not what you wanted to hear."

"I agree. Don't be so careless," Leah said.

I put my head in my arms and sighed. When I sat up, I heard someone say, "Yeah, that seems like the best idea."

"What does?" I said quickly.

My mom turned to me. "I'll go with you to visit Declan's group. We can decide what the best course of action is from there."

I sighed, but I knew they were right. I nodded my head slightly.

"This can't be happening," my dad said quietly.

I opened my mouth to protest, but quickly shut it. Truth was, I didn't know what was happening. I glanced out the window and thought I saw a shadow move in the backyard. I shivered.

Before my birthday, I would've dismissed it as a stray animal. But now, I knew it wasn't.

NINE

That night, I dreamt of her again. Another night of broken sleep, of waiting to hear the sound of breaking glass, of my name being called in the darkness. Of expecting the Octavians to pull me from my bed.

But, finally, exhaustion took over and I slept. The dream came quickly.

I was in what looked like a courtyard of the palace. I sat on white limestone steps that lead down to a pool of water with brightly colored fish swimming in it. It was nighttime, though, and the grounds were mostly empty, save for a few soldiers patrolling the perimeter.

My hair fell long and straight across my shoulders, and I wore a simple linen tunic that looked like a nightgown.

On my lap was the Book of the Dead that the scribe had given me.

The scroll was open, and it shimmered in front of me as though waving hello. The delicate black and red script wavered back and forth before solidifying. I ran my finger lightly across the hieroglyphs on the crinkly papyrus and felt a jolt, like static electricity. I glanced up at the soldiers, but they didn't seem to have seen anything.

I touched it again, the surface crackling beneath my fingertips. At the top was a row of eyes, which slowly blinked at me the same way the scribe did when he'd handed me the Book. They each had a lightning-bolt stream of tears falling from them, like the tattoo.

Underneath the row of eyes was an illustration of a woman sitting on a throne, a long staff in her right hand. On the top of the staff was a pair of golden wings, like the wings that flowed from the woman's back. She looked human, but totally not human all at the same time. On her head was a ceremonial headdress of white and black, and her long black hair flowed from underneath it.

I leaned in closer and stared at her face. Something about her features looked familiar. The eyes, the way they tipped up at the corners. And then, I realized.

It was me.

Underneath the drawing was a symbol. It looked like a cross but the top part was a circle. As I touched it, I remembered seeing the image before, in the museum. It was an ankh, a symbol for eternal life, associated with the gods.

As I slowly traced it, my fingertips awoke again and a rush of powerful magic swept through my arm, settling around my heart. I lifted my shaking hand and saw that my fingers were glowing, first white, then red.

Again, no one seemed to notice the magic. It was only for me to see. I looked up into the sky and saw a brilliant spray of stars, including one pink one that seemed to twinkle directly above my head.

"My lady, you should get some rest."

I jumped up, the Book falling from my lap, to see a lady-in-waiting staring at me, a concerned look on her face.

I nodded and followed her toward the palace. The scents of jasmine and saltwater overwhelmed me as we climbed the stairs to my bedchamber. I turned around and saw, in the distance, the moon glittering off the Mediterranean Sea.

"Beautiful," I murmured.

The lady-in-waiting nodded in agreement. "Yes, but you must rest. The High Priestess is coming tomorrow to deliver a message to you." Something about the way her eyes sparkled when she said this made my pulse quicken.

And then, I woke up.

I gasped awake in my bedroom, my breath caught in huge heaving swallows in my throat. My fingers still burned from touching the Book, even though it was only in my dream. But my veins were pulsing, like magic still coursed through them.

TEN

"Watch your step," Declan said, in front of me.

I saw the orange traffic cone just in time and stepped aside, avoiding the puddle of water that seemed to have dripped from the ceiling. I stood near Declan as we waited for the elevator and glanced around. This definitely wasn't what I'd expected when I'd agreed to visit the Order of Antony's command center. I pictured us having to spelunk through some dark cave with gas-powered lanterns, battling giant spiders as we wound through passages made of dirt and worms. Then, we'd have to recite some secret word or phrase to gain access to the lair.

Instead, we were in an office building not far from where my mom grocery shops. Other than having to wave a blank white ID card in front of the gate guarding the parking lot, there definitely weren't any secret codes to crack.

My mom was waiting outside in her Buick, at my request. I needed to see everything by myself—not as some kid on a field trip with her mother.

Declan and I rode the elevator to the third floor and stepped out. He pushed open the wood door to a suite labeled *OoA, Inc.*

"Sorry, I know this place doesn't look like much, but we didn't have much time to set down roots after Duat appeared and we found you," Declan said. I nodded and followed him inside.

A secretary, whose black and gray hair was pulled back at the nape of her neck, sat at a desk looking bored. "Welcome back, Mr. Declan," she said without looking up.

He cleared his throat and the secretary glanced up. She stared at me with a blank look on her face.

"This is Rhea Spencer," Declan said.

I shifted uncomfortably and glanced back at the door.

"Oh. Okay. Hello, Ms. Spencer," the secretary said. She turned back to her computer and started pecking at it, muttering about an email glitch.

I laughed and Declan rolled his eyes. "She's new," he said. I followed him through basic hallways covered in gray carpeting and cream wallpaper until we got to a conference room with a long wooden table in the center of it. I imagined the other members of the Order were sitting in boring cubicles and drumming their fingers.

"Everyone else should be here soon," he said.

I sighed as I sat down in one of the chairs and glanced at my watch. I was hoping to be in and out of this place quickly and back home as soon as possible. Although I wasn't sleeping well, I still didn't want to stay there. It wasn't that I didn't think the danger was real...I was just never a hide-and-seek kind of girl. Besides, being holed up in this office with Declan, the secretary, and a bunch of other random guys didn't exactly sound appealing.

"So, is this your full-time job?" I asked.

"I'm a college student—or at least I was until a few weeks ago. I came up here when I heard from the Order that the prophecy was coming true." Declan spoke quickly, his words spilling out like he'd been rehearsing it.

"How did you get involved in all of this in the first place?" I said, picking at my nails.

Declan didn't look at me. "My parents were involved in the Order. I'm just following in their footsteps."

"Are they here?" I looked around the conference room as if I expected them to appear.

"They're dead," he said shortly. "I was raised by my uncle."

"Oh. I'm sorry." I waited for him to say more about his family, but he just sat there quietly. He looked relieved when three other guys walked in. One, with thick blond hair and a body like an NFL player, looked like he was in his late twenties. The other two men—who looked amazingly alike—were older, probably in their thirties.

"Rhea, this is John." Declan pointed to the blond guy.

"And Curt and Luther." He pointed to the twins. "And this, gentlemen, is Rhea Spencer."

They all nodded hello and stared at me. "What's up?" I finally said, with a lame half-wave. I felt like I was the cross between a celebrity, a show pony, and a stalking victim. I shifted uncomfortably in the rolling chair.

Declan's coworkers sat down at the table, never taking their eyes off of me. I suppose it was strange for them, after hearing about me for so many years, to now see me sitting there wearing ripped jeans and a black tank top. My hair was curly and long against my back, scrunched into waves. Maybe they'd expected me to walk into the office wearing a gold headdress or thick black eyeliner, with long straight black hair.

"Are you sure this is her?" John, the blond guy, hissed at Declan. Declan shot him a dirty look and nodded.

"Nice," I muttered. I wanted to spit out that they didn't look too secret society-ish themselves and maybe they should put on some white robes and start doing weird chants to convince me of their membership.

"Rhea," Declan began. He clasped his hands on the table in front of him and I did the same. "As I told you before, the Order of Antony is an ancient order that has been around since the first century BC. We were formed by Mark Antony himself, before his death, to ensure that Cleopatra's legacy was in the correct hands. Cleopatra always knew that her soul would be reincarnated, and she wanted her future self to be protected—and that included her Book of the Dead."

"The Order has been waiting a long time for you," Luther said quietly. "And so have the Octavians."

A shiver ran down my spine. The thought of a whole group of people—of this whole place, this whole society—being formed because of me, and watching me, was both strangely flattering and totally creepy.

"As I've said before, it is our position as the Order of Antony that you should entrust us with your safety and allow us to hide you here, out of sight of the Octavians. We can protect you while we work to get the Book away from them. We've discovered that they've taken it to their headquarters, which are located in the basement of a museum in Alexandria. We don't know exactly where in the headquarters they're keeping it, but we're developing intel about this. Once we locate the Book, we'll devise a plan to steal it. It shouldn't take more than a couple of months for it to be returned to you."

I looked at him, startled. He'd never mentioned bringing the Book here, to me. "You want me to have the Book?"

Curt cleared his throat. "Rhea, only the true owner of the Book—the one it was created for—can read it. The spells contained in it will enable you to wield a control-the-world type of magic. That's why the Octavians want you so badly. But there's also an escape clause—a spell in the Book that will destroy it forever."

"So you want to bring it to me so I can say the spell to destroy it forever?"

Declan interrupted me. "That's the general idea, but we have to get the Book first. For now, will you agree to remain here for your safety, at least during your summer vacation?"

I scrunched my face up and tried to look like I was contemplating their offer, but given Declan's expression, I think I just looked confused.

"Thanks for the offer, but I still want to stay at home, even with everything that's happened. I don't feel like I can just leave my life behind." A little voice in the back of my head reminded me that Slade might not be around to protect me in the future, thanks to his upcoming kingship, but I swallowed hard and brushed that thought out of my head. "Really, I'll be fine."

"I disagree," John said. He gazed pointedly at my still-bandaged arm resting on the table.

I quickly shoved my arm out of sight and shook my head. "Look, it's my decision."

Declan rubbed his forehead, looking pained. "Stubborn. Just like the queen herself." He looked back at me, his eyes pleading. "You were attacked. This is much bigger than any of us, and we can't keep you safe if you're not here. That's been proven."

I chewed the inside of my cheek and looked down.

"Regardless of whether you stay here or not, you'll need

to come here to train," Curt said. His voice was black and flat.

"Train? For what?" I was half-standing, ready to leave, and plopped back down into my chair. It rolled away from the table a little.

Curt looked at Declan. "Really? You didn't tell her about this yet?"

Declan shook his head and sighed. Something in his eyes made my stomach drop.

"What have you guys been keeping from me?" I asked, my voice shaking.

Curt scratched a pencil on a piece of paper and slid it toward me. It was an ankh symbol, like the one I'd seen in the Book in my dream.

"The goddess of Isis," Declan said quietly.

I narrowed my eyes at him.

"Cleopatra was the human form of the goddess Isis." His blue eyes softened. "And so are you."

ELEVEN

Ten days later, and the news that I apparently had the powers of a goddess still didn't compute. I certainly didn't feel like a goddess or anything close to it. My parents were worried that I hadn't taken the Order up on their offer, but they'd agreed to let me come home rather than stay at the compound. Of course, this meant that I was almost never alone, but at least my companions were my sisters and Slade rather than Declan and his buddies.

So it had taken a lot of fast talking to get my family to even let me have dinner with Slade's parents, but they'd finally, reluctantly agreed. I felt as unmagical as ever as I sat around the table with Slade's Créatúir family.

"Why aren't you eating? Don't you like the food?" Slade's

mother, Caiside, asked. She gazed at me, her purple eyes glowing a little against her light blue skin.

I smiled. "It's very good." I lifted a forkful of—well, I don't know what it was. All I knew was that it was a plate of meat that looked like a cross between a chewed-up hamburger and a rat's tail. I forced myself to take a tiny bite, willing down the waves of nausea that begged me to spit it out and hightail it out of there.

We'd agreed to meet at the Kerry Piper, a Créatúir club and restaurant on the outskirts of town. It looked like any regular Irish bar from the outside, but the inside was all disco balls, black wine goblets, and red velvet banquet seating. In the center of the club was a giant black statue of a naked, winged centaur. I wondered what our elderly neighbors would think if I dragged it home and left it on the front lawn.

Although, to be honest, I would've rather had dinner with those neighbors, who scowled at me from their front porch every morning, than Slade's parents. When I'd extended my hand to greet his mom, she'd quickly stepped backward and looked at me as if I'd just tried to feel her up.

"Mmmm." Caiside made a disapproving sound and glanced down at my full plate, then looked me over for the millionth time before glancing at her husband. I tried to keep my face neutral and pretend I didn't notice her stares, but I really wanted to give both of them the finger. I hadn't expected a warm and fuzzy welcome, but the woman could have at least pretended to like me, and then talked about me behind my back like a normal person.

Slade nudged my leg under the table and gave me a sympathetic look. He knew this was the last thing I wanted to do right now, but we'd made these plans forever ago and I wasn't about to let any Egyptian drama or Octavians stand in my way. Not to mention that we had an ulterior motive for this dinner.

Keep it together.

I took a deep breath. "It really is nice to finally meet you." I smiled as brilliantly as I could and hoped that some of my Cleopatra charm would work on them. But apparently Cleopatra's influence didn't extend to the Créatúir, since Slade's father absentmindedly nodded and said something to his mother in Créatúir-speak.

Great. Talking in their own language again. Not a good sign.

The language of Slade's homeland always sounded like a cross between a growl and a scream. His parents stopped mid-sentence to give me disapproving looks, then continued talking.

Slade interrupted them in English. "You know, Rhea is a very important person in the human realm."

My head snapped toward him and my eyes grew wide. We did not plan on telling them anything about Cleopatra or my supposed goddess-ness. Especially since it wasn't something I'd been able to wrap my mind around yet.

"Thus," Slade continued, giving me a quick look, "I was

hoping for your permission to bring her to the Other Realm for a small period of time. To—to show her how wonderful our world is." His words broke off at the end, and it was probably the least convincing sentence ever spoken.

Slade's parents looked at each other and spoke in their own language again, but this time it was high-pitched and urgent. I sighed and looked at Slade. He was listening, his face drawn.

Suddenly, the chatter stopped and Slade's dad, Eraidon, looked at me. I held my breath and waited. "No," he said. Then, he turned back to his wife and started speaking again.

"I don't need your permission, you know," Slade said. He put his palms on the table and stared his parents down.

"Slade—" I started, but he waved me off.

"She needs our help, my protection. I can keep her safe in our world, away from those who are trying to kidnap her," Slade said quietly.

Slade's mom opened her mouth, revealing tiny, rabbit-like teeth, and let out a roar. Smiling, she said something to Slade.

Awesome. She's totally laughing at me.

I couldn't translate what she was saying—Leah is the only one who can do that—but I was pretty sure she said something like, "Why would anyone want to kidnap *her*?"

Then Caiside turned to me. "Our son is going to be king. He doesn't have time for a human. Much less…you." She gave me one final once-over to punctuate her point.

I clenched my fists in my lap to prevent myself from taking a swing at her. "I'm royalty!" I blurted out. "And possibly a goddess, too. Am I good enough now?"

I knew I sounded like a four-year-old having a tantrum; it was almost like I was floating above my body, shaking my head in shame at the ridiculously childish things I was saying, but I had no control.

Slade sighed and put his head in his hands. For a moment, no one spoke—Créatúir or human. Caiside looked at me hard, her eyes narrowed. She tapped the table with her long, green fingernails. Then she turned and nodded at Eraidon. He glanced behind himself, at the bartender, who walked to the front door of the empty restaurant and opened it.

I felt a gust of warm air from the summer night as a group of men rushed in and surrounded the table. About ten huge, burly guys—all dressed in black from head to toe, wearing black leather cuff bracelets with spikes on their right arms—stared us down.

"What's going on?" I said, noticing that they were all eyeing me like I was dinner.

Octavians.

"What did you do, Mother?" Slade asked quietly.

Caiside ignored him and trained her eyes on Eraidon. They spoke in Créatúir-speak, softly, and then looked at me.

I felt a cold, hard point dig into my neck. One of the burly guys said, "Let's go, sweetheart."

I started to jerk away, but he dug the knifepoint a little

harder into my skin and I yelped in pain. I felt a warm stream of blood run down onto my collarbone.

"Get off of her!" Slade yelled, trying to stand up. The burly guys put their hands on his shoulders and pushed him down, but he disappeared and then reappeared behind the knife guy. I felt a rustle and the knife dug deeper into my neck.

"Slade, stop!" I screamed. Tears started to run down my cheeks. I looked at Slade's parents, who were watching everything with calm, neutral expressions. "You set me up? How could you?"

"I'm sorry. It is the only way to ensure the success of my son's kingship. You are the only thing that could cause problems for us," Caiside said to me. She turned to her son. "They won't hurt her. They gave us their word."

"But HOW could you? How did you know about all of this?" I shrieked. The guy holding the knife so roughly grabbed my arm—the one still healing from the glass—and forced me to a standing position.

Caiside chuckled again. "There is very little that goes on in your world that we do not see." She leaned forward. "And don't forget, your sister Leah is watched very closely by all of us. Everything you tell her, we hear." She waved her hand around. "They just want to talk to her," she said to Slade. "It's really not a big deal."

Slade shifted again, behind his mother, and placed his hands around her neck.

"I wouldn't if I were you," Caiside said icily. "You know the consequences. You will be thrown into a Glancaugh circle if you kill a member of the royal family." She reached forward and casually sipped her tea.

Slade's hands dropped to his sides and he looked helplessly at me. I couldn't blame him—while I didn't know everything about the Créatúir, I knew a Glancaugh circle was something like a never-ending labyrinth. Not a very pleasant way to spend eternity.

"They won't hurt her," Caiside said again.

"You have no idea what you've done. They lied to you," Slade hissed at her.

One of the Octavians stepped in front of me and roughly grabbed my wrists, binding them with a plastic tie. I'd never thought that this was how it would all end. I'd even told Declan and the Order not to follow me tonight, since the magic at the Kerry Piper wouldn't allow them to enter anyway. I figured I would be safe with Slade—which I would have been, had his evil mother not sold me for some magic beans.

"And just to be sure you don't try to run," the burly guy in front of me said as he reached behind him, "I have this." He stretched his arm out and on his forearm was a red, black, and white snake. It hissed at me and opened its mouth wide, revealing fangs dripping with venom. I shrank and stumbled backward, falling over a chair and onto the ground.

The Octavians laughed. One brought the snake closer

to me as Slade stood helplessly behind his parents. "Now, you behave, or else we'll throw you in a cage with our little pet here." He nodded to his friends and they began to head toward the door. He turned to grab me and lead me outside.

I knew I couldn't let them drag me away from the club. It would all be over. I would be dead ... or worse.

I opened my mouth and screamed, a guttural, feral sound that I didn't know I could make. I felt my blood rush through my veins as I heaped all of my fear, anxiety, and pain into that sound.

The ground started to rumble. At first it felt like a minor earthquake, as the water glasses clinked and the plates started to dance across the table. It continued, amping up in intensity, and the bottles behind the bar started to fall and shatter. The bartender ran for cover just before a rack of glasses crashed forward and sent jagged spikes of glass across the club.

"What's going on?" one of the Octavians said. His legs had tiny cuts on them from the falling glass.

There was a loud crack and the floor of the club split into two—first a hairline fracture, and then a gaping hole about a foot wide.

I skittered away from the separating earth, and Slade rushed over and pulled me toward him. And then the shaking stopped.

"What is THAT?" another Octavian shouted. He pointed to the crack, where a bluish, peeling, rotting appendage was slowly extending upward. It was covered in black fur stained with blood, and it had pale blue eyes.

I stared in horror as the thing crawled out of the crack and stood next to me as though waiting for a command. As I shrank against Slade, I realized it was a dog—or, at least, it used to be.

"What the HELL is that?" the Octavian shouted again. They stared at the dog and one of them took a step toward me, but the dog growled and revealed bloodstained teeth. The Octavians backed up, hands in the air.

"Did you know she could do that?" one of the Octavians asked another, who shook his head.

"Get out of here or I'll make some more!" I screamed, even though I wasn't sure exactly what I had done. The dog certainly appeared dead, but had I really called it up?

The zombie dog leaned his head back and let out a horrible moan, like a thousand pieces of antique furniture all creaking at the same time. My would-be kidnappers scattered out the door, promising to return. I turned to Slade's parents, but they had already vanished—shifted back into their world. We were alone; even the bartender was gone.

I stared down the dog, who wagged his tail and gave me a doggie smile. I frowned and stepped back, afraid to get too close.

"What just happened?" I whispered. The dog smiled wider at my voice and trotted over to sit on my foot.

"Where did that thing come from?" Slade said. He tried to pull me away, but the dog just scooted closer to me.

"Um, thanks. You can go back into that crack, to the grave or whatever." I pointed to the separation in the floor and nodded my head, but the dog just whined and scratched at my leg with a decaying paw. "Great. Always wanted a family pet. Hope you get along with Doppler," I muttered.

And then, I leaned against Slade, closed my eyes, and cried.

☥
TWELVE

I'm guessing that thing isn't up to date on its rabies shot," Declan said as he backed slowly away from Zombo the zombie dog.

"Trust me, rabies is the last thing you should be worrying about." I glanced down at my newly acquired, unwanted pet. "Go 'way. Get!" I waved my hands around at him, but he just snuggled closer to my leg. I sighed. "He's basically my shadow."

I'd tried running away from him and telling him to go fetch, and I'd even considered dropping him off at the pound and running, but he remained my mini sidekick. A very dead, gross sidekick. He had saved my life, though, so despite his unpleasant odor I was developing a fondness for him—decay and all.

Declan put his hands in front of him, to show Zombo that he meant no harm—not that the dog cared, he was too busy attaching himself to my leg—and slowly sat down at the conference table in the Order's office building. After the dead-dog-raising incident, I'd gone straight there. Slade wanted to come with me, but he had to go to the Other Realm to discuss his kingship training activities. It was just as well. I knew it wasn't his fault that his parents had essentially sold me out, but I needed to be alone. Away from all things Créatúir and clear my head.

"Did you know I could do this?" I asked, gesturing to the dog.

Declan looked at me for a long time before answering. "No. Absolutely not. Well, that's not entirely true. It's well known that Isis was sort of a mother to all things undead, but we had no idea you could raise the dead just by feeling stressed."

"Oh, great. So you're telling me I might get stuck with a bunch of corpses follow me around any time I get stressed out?" I threw myself into a chair and pressed my cheek against the cool wood table. This was completely out of hand.

"We don't really know what you're capable of, Rhea." Declan's voice was quiet and serious, so I switched to my other cheek and stared at him.

"Why hasn't this power of mine come out before?" I said.

Declan laced his fingers in front of him and sighed. "We

don't really know. It's obviously related to you turning six-teen and the appearance of the star Duat. I'm sorry, but we just don't have all the answers." He stood up, walked over to me, and awkwardly patted me on the back. His touch was oddly comforting, despite the decaying canine resting on my feet.

"If I have all this power now, what's the big deal about the Book?" I asked.

"Well, the Book of the Dead was the most sacred text in Ancient Egyptian times," Declan replied. "You may have innate abilities that come out when you're stressed, but the Book of the Dead holds the key to unlocking your true potential. You're not actually supposed to be able to raise the dead or perform any magic without the Book." He stopped patting. "If the Octavians succeed in kidnapping you, there's no telling what could happen."

"Great," I muttered into my arm.

"I implore you again to stay here. With us. We will keep you safe until all this is over."

I turned toward the table and closed my eyes. Staying there would mean giving up all my freedom. I'd be watched constantly, followed around by guys who looked like Secret Service members. Whenever a new president was elected, I always thought about his kids, how awful it would be to have constant babysitters. It would be like grounding, times a thousand.

But I knew I had to make the decision soon. If I continued to risk everything, I'd be deader than Zombo.

Or worse.

―――――――

The next morning the house was quiet when I woke. "Mom, Dad?" I called as I walked out of my bedroom. I didn't see anyone, but could faintly hear Gia's laugh from across the house. "Gia, where are you?" I yelled.

"In here!" she answered. I followed her voice and found her sitting on the floor in front of the television. "Look at this." She pointed to the screen. "It's a video of all of us from Halloween, like ten years ago."

I sank down on my knees next to my little sister and watched the screen. My sisters and I—Morgana at eight, Leah at seven, me at six, and Gia at five—were all dancing around in the backyard, dressed up as angels. I remembered protesting about wanting to go as something different from my sisters, but my mom had insisted. So I wore shiny red patent leather shoes underneath my Halloween costume and told everyone I was a fallen angel.

My sisters and I waved to the camera. Gia smiled brilliantly, Morgana put her arm around us, Leah stared off in the distance—probably at some random Créatúir—and I stuck my tongue out and made my "monster face."

"Girls, girls! Do you like Halloween?" I heard my mother ask from behind the camera.

"Yes!" we all shouted.

"C'mon ladies, let's go trick-or-treating." My dad appeared in the frame, looking much younger with more hair and way less of it gray. "Just no tricks!" He tried to scoop all of us up into his arms, but we shrieked and ran away. The last shot before the camera faded away was my dad chasing us around the yard.

"Do you remember that?" Gia asked.

I made a noise and quickly brushed away the tears that had formed. I swallowed quickly, trying to will away the lump in my throat.

"Hey, what happened?" Gia leaned forward and lightly touched the spot on my neck where the burly guy had held the knife.

"Oh, nothing. I fell down," I said quickly. I'd planned on telling my family what happened, but I couldn't tell Gia. Even at fifteen, she seemed so young and innocent. Besides, I knew it would upset her too much.

"Well—hey!" She pointed to the window. "There's a dog out there."

"I'm sure there is," I muttered. Sure enough, Zombo was sitting outside the living room window, whining to be let in the house.

"He looks sick or something. Do you think we should call someone?" Gia asked. She walked over to the window and knelt down. Zombo wagged his tail. "He seems kind of friendly."

"You have no idea," I said. I smiled as Gia scampered off to tell my mom about the "sick dog" outside. My eyes drifted to the window again, but this time, they focused just behind Zombo, at a dark shadow that moved on the sidewalk.

It was the Octavian who'd held the knife to my throat in the Kerry Piper. He was staring at me, a small smile on his face. My pulse pounded as I considered my options. There was no way I could run away; he would grab me the moment I left the house. But I wasn't strong enough to fight him if he came inside. Declan and the Order wouldn't be able to get here in time.

But then, his gaze shifted to another window of the house. He watched intently, and then smiled a little broader before drawing a long finger against his throat. He was staring at the window of my parents' bedroom—a window where he could probably see my mom and Gia.

Suddenly, I had a horrible thought—a vision, but not like my visions of Cleopatra. It was of the Octavians grabbing my sisters and holding knives to their necks until they bled, of them screaming until I agreed to cooperate.

I knew I couldn't stay at my house anymore without putting everyone—my family—in more danger. I knew what I had to do.

So when my mother walked in the room to see the "sick dog," I closed my eyes and said, "I'm not safe here."

THIRTEEN

You'll be just fine here, sweetheart," my dad said as he surveyed my bedroom at the Order's headquarters. I'd assumed I would be sleeping on some conference room table, but Declan showed us a whole back section to the building, which had rooms for the Order members and one reserved for me. He told us that after they'd found office space, their first task was setting up a room in case I agreed to stay with them.

It was a week after I'd seen the Octavian in my parents' backyard; I'd told everyone from school that I was going to Paris for the summer to visit a cousin. Harper and Reagan had squealed with jealousy and made me promise to bring them back all kinds of souvenirs, which I figured I'd have to order off the Internet to back up my story. But it was worth it—not only would I be in danger if I continued living at home, but I was putting everyone else in harm's way too, and that was almost too much to handle. If anything ever happened to my family—especially because of me—I just couldn't imagine living.

Still, it felt like I'd agreed to be shipped off to a messed-up boarding school.

At first, my dad was worried about me leaving, but he eventually came around after realizing it was only temporary; Declan had assured him it would only take a couple of months for the Order to take care of the threat. Dad saw how secure the compound was, and was told many, many times over that any family member could have full access to me whenever they wanted. And that Slade wouldn't be allowed any late-night visits.

"I love you and all I care about is that you're safe, okay?" my dad said. I nodded and he pulled me toward him in a bear hug. My cheek crushed against his starchy policeman's uniform.

"Your spirit will guide you every step of the way," my mother murmured into my ear. I hugged her next, and my sisters gathered around and embraced me in a huge circle.

"Just think of it like a cool hotel," Morgana said. "Before you know it, you'll be home and everything will be back to normal. And I bet you won't have to take out any trash here."

I managed a small smile. "Whatever will I do with all the free time?"

"We'll come back soon and hang out, okay?" Gia said. Leah nodded, but she didn't say anything. I knew she was blaming herself for what had happened with Slade's parents. It's not like it was her fault, but I could tell she'd felt bad when she heard about it, like everything the Créatúir did was her responsibility.

"Sounds good," I told them lightly as they shuffled out of my room.

I closed the door behind my family and surveyed my new digs. It really did look like a hotel room—with a television, a big fluffy white bed, and a nightstand. The bathroom was a simple shower and sink, but I didn't have to share it with three sisters so things were already looking up.

Could be worse, I thought to myself. My dad had forced us to go camping a few years ago, and we all slept in one of those pop-up trailers. Morgana snored, and Gia got up to go to the bathroom like a thousand times. That was way worse than this, I was sure.

I heard scratching at the door and peered out the peephole, my heart racing.

Ugh. Of course.

I cracked open the door and let Zombo trot in. He settled in the corner on my suitcase and quickly fell asleep.

And that's how the first night of the rest of my life began—just me and a zombie dog.

FOURTEEN

The next day, I was ready to settle in with the Order. I was told that my training would begin with a few days of studying history so I could get a framework for Cleopatra, and then we'd work on learning hieroglyphs and reading about the gods and goddesses, so that when it came time for me to destroy the Book, I'd know exactly which spell to look for.

"So, how much do you know about Cleopatra?" Declan asked as I tucked myself into an overstuffed black velvet chair in the compound's screening room.

I shrugged. "Just the basics—became queen of Egypt, had an affair with Julius Caesar and then one with Mark Antony, killed herself with a snake rather than be taken prisoner by the Romans." It sounded so pathetic when I said it.

I *should* know more about her, but I'd spent so long either pretending that I wasn't her or wishing I had a different gift—one like my sisters'—that I hadn't spent much time reading about her life. Besides, I never thought that knowing more about her would change my life in any real way. Clearly, I was wrong.

Curt and Luther shot me annoyed looks. "We certainly have our work cut out for us," Luther grumbled.

Learning about Cleopatra's history had sounded interesting at first, but now it was quickly taking on the vibe of the SAT. I once saw this news special on how children in other countries are drilled on academics for hours each day, practically from birth. I assumed that must be less intense than being interrogated by the Order.

"Why don't we just show her the visuals?" Curt motioned to a projector on the side of the room. "It would be so much easier."

Declan considered me for a minute, then nodded. He opened a gold case and plucked out a pair of black sunglasses and handed them to me. "Put these on."

"What is this? Are we going to watch a 3-D movie?"

"Something like that." He nodded and clicked a button on the projector.

"Great. I'd rather see things for myself anyway." I thought I heard a chuckle, but I couldn't see anything with the glasses on. "Where is the screen? I don't—"

Suddenly the room flashed white and Declan and I were

standing together, alone, on a sand dune that stretched all the way to the horizon.

"Huh?" I said, turning around and around.

"It's more than a 3-D movie—it's like a virtual reality presentation," Declan said. "Ready?"

I nodded, and he clicked something on a remote in his hand. We were instantly in the throne room from my dream, standing behind Cleopatra's tall gold chair. The same scribe was kneeling in front of her, offering the Book of the Dead. It was the first time I had *seen* Cleopatra from the outside, as a three-dimensional person. My heart began to pound as I studied her face.

She had high cheekbones and skin the color of light caramel. Her nose was strong and balanced, her jawline firm. Her eyes were wide and dark, but glittered with wisdom and serenity. On her head was a white ribbon, and, sewn into her jet black hair, were beautiful pink pearls. She wore a simple white caftan, but a wide gold belt encrusted with rubies and diamonds glittered around her waist. A foot peeked out from under her caftan and I saw that her sandals were encrusted with jewels, too.

"She looks so different than me, yet just what I expected," I said.

We watched the scene as the scribe with the tattoo gave the Book to Cleopatra. "What's with this tattoo again?" I asked.

Declan reached a hand up and self-consciously patted

his neck. "It's a symbol for the Order of Antony. Mark Antony formed the society after the Donations of Alexandria. He'd made a big public display of gifting Roman lands to Cleopatra and her children. Only... they weren't his to give away, and so the Romans got pretty upset about it. There was a lot of public and civil unrest, so he formed the Order to always protect her." Declan gave me a long look before continuing. "He knew he would probably be murdered, but he wanted Cleopatra to be safe no matter what. We have offices all over the world, since we didn't know where the queen's soul would reappear."

The throne room scene faded away quickly and we were suddenly on the edge of a river, palm trees and grass all around us.

"The Nile," Declan said. "That's Mark Antony." He pointed to a man and woman sitting on the river bank. Mark Antony's arms were wrapped around Cleopatra. A lump formed in my throat as I thought of Slade, but I quickly pushed him out of my mind. Even after he became king, we would stay together. I just felt it.

The queen leaned into his embrace as Mark Antony slowly ran his hand down her arm and laced his fingers through hers. He whispered something in her ear, and she closed her eyes and smiled.

"They knew their existence in this lifetime was limited. They had too many enemies, so they promised to reincarnate together," Declan said quietly. "We have secret papyrus scrolls that were exchanged between the two of them, in which they pledge to return from the Underworld together. She knew she could make it happen through her powers as Isis."

"What?" My heart began to beat faster. "A pledge to return? So who is..." I gave him a startled look and felt my face begin to flush. "Are you?"

I didn't need to finish my sentence, since Declan started shaking his head violently. "No. Not me," he said. "We don't know if Antony ever reincarnated, but that's not important. What's important is that we get the Book from the Octavians so that you can destroy it."

Cleopatra and Mark raised their palms and placed them together. A soft white light appeared between them.

"Her powers, gifted from Isis. She rarely showed them to anyone," Declan said. "I think he was the only one."

Cleopatra reached over and touched a dying flower, which quickly sprouted and came to life. "She had the power to reanimate the dead," Declan said.

"Mmmm hmmm," I murmured, thinking of Zombo trapped in my room, whining and pacing for more hot dogs. Gia had given him one the first night he stayed at our house, and it was almost like he'd died again and gone to heaven.

Then everything went black, and we were suddenly standing on a street. But not just any street—it had to be at least a hundred feet wide and was surrounded by tall white buildings on either side. In the distance, I could see the sparkling sea and an island in the harbor, with a huge lighthouse to greet ships. To the right was a massive temple with huge gold pillars framing the entrance. On either side of the doorway there were carvings and paintings of Cleopatra.

"The Pharos Lighthouse and the Temple of Isis," Declan said, following my gaze.

I was so entranced by the view, I didn't notice at first that we were surrounded by a crowd of people.

Mark Antony lay dying in the street, blood seeping from a wound in his stomach. Cleopatra knelt next to him, screaming as the blood soaked through her white robe. Tears ran down her face and tracked black rivers across her cheeks. Her hair frizzed out of her braids as she pulled at them, feral screams coming from her chest. The Egyptians around her murmured but looked unfazed at the display. Then a group of men appeared at Cleopatra's side, and she stood and nodded. They walked toward Antony's body and began to lift it. I noticed they all had the Order's tattoos.

"They're taking him for burial," Declan said.

Cleopatra bent down and lightly kissed Mark Antony, then whispered in his ear in Egyptian. I made an effort not to make a face. I felt Declan studying me, trying to determine if I'd heard what she said, but I kept my expression neutral.

"How sad," I said quickly.

We were back in the screening room, and I quickly pulled the sunglasses off my face. "Does it make more sense now?" Declan asked.

I nodded. "They were in love, but they were doomed.

So they promised to come back together, and Antony knew the Order would protect her after he was dead."

Declan nodded.

There was a pause. I'd learned everything about Cleopatra and the forming of the Order, but I still hadn't heard a piece of history that interested me. "You still haven't really told me how you got involved. I know you said it was through your parents or something, but what's the story there?"

Declan shifted in his chair and looked at the ground for a minute. I braced myself for another silence, but he answered me. "My mom was a famous archaeologist, interested in Egyptology. Well"—he head cocked to the side and a faraway look crossed his eyes—"obsessed is probably a better description. She fell in love with my dad, whose family had been involved in the Order for centuries. They traveled all over the world together, excavating sites and sleeping in tents. She was like the female version of Indiana Jones."

He paused and I waited for him to continue, but he was quiet. "So what happened to them?" I said softly.

Declan cleared his throat and shook his head. "Plane crash near Dubrovnik when I was five."

I thought of my sisters and who wondered who would raise us if anything happened to our parents. "Did you have any brothers or sisters?" I asked.

He gave me a quick look and then stood up. "A brother."

"Is he—" I started, but he quickly turned toward the door.

"Let me know if you have any questions about what we learned in our session," he said before the door closed behind him.

I was used to getting blocked. Slade had practically perfected it as an art form. But there was such sadness behind Declan's voice that I wondered just what he had been through—and maybe what he had given up for all of this. I swallowed quickly, a lump forming in my throat, and walked back toward my room. I pushed thoughts of Declan out of my mind and tried to focus on Cleopatra.

I thought back to that final scene, where Mark Antony died in her arms. She'd said, "We will meet again."

FIFTEEN

The next day, I took a long walk around the Order's building. Since I was a willing hostage, I made it a point to go outside each day and at least stroll around the neighborhood. It consisted of little more than suburban strip malls, asphalt parking lots, and occasional manmade corporate ponds with limp fountains in the middle. I'd expected my first "real" summer vacation to be filled with parties and lying out at Harper's pool while drinking ice-cold lemonade. Instead, I was shuffling around an office park with a bodyguard-like member of the Order trailing behind me. I'd left Zombo in my room, although he wasn't thrilled about leaving my side for a decaying second.

As I returned—there were only so many times I could circle around the post office box in the parking lot—I saw

Slade sitting outside the building. "Hey! What are you doing here?" I called. I hadn't seen him since I'd moved in with the Order; he'd been in the Other Realm again training for his kingship. "I thought we weren't going to see each other for another few days."

Slade stood up, and I noticed the dark expression on his face. He glanced over my shoulder at Curt, who was lingering on the sidewalk pretending he wasn't trying to listen to our conversation.

"Give us a few minutes, okay?" I called to Curt. "You can still watch me from inside."

Curt nodded and stepped inside the building, staring at me through the glass window. "Being on lockdown sure is fun," I muttered. I mustered up a smile and looked up at Slade. "Good to see you."

He leaned down and kissed me quickly before stepping back.

Uh oh.

"What's wrong?" I said, shoving my hands into my pockets. I started to sweat even though the temperature was only in the seventies.

Slade ran a hand through his long hair and then looked at his palm for a minute, as if studying it. "I need to remember all of this," he said quietly.

My heart began to race. "What do you mean? Remember what?"

He slowly looked back at me, his violet eyes soft, and

pulled me toward him. "I've been summoned. To be king. Queen Kiera stepped down sooner than expected."

I bit down on the corner of my lip, hard. "That's—that's great. Congratulations." I swallowed all of the things I wanted to do—beg him not to go, scream that it wasn't fair, ask why he wasn't turning it down. Force him to say exactly what being king would mean for us.

But I really wasn't in a position to question anything. I couldn't figure my own life out. I was in total crisis mode myself.

Slade shook his head slightly. "You don't understand. When I become king, I'll need to stay in my world. For good."

I stepped back quickly and stumbled a little over a crack in the sidewalk. I saw Curt start toward the door but I held my hand out. "So what does that mean?" I knew exactly what that meant, but he didn't get to just walk away without saying it. He had to be the one to say the words.

Slade held his hand out, palm up. A soft light appeared in the center. I shook my head and turned away. "Say it," I said. He wasn't going to get any comfort from me.

He curled his hand back down to his side. "We can't be together anymore," he whispered. He sat down on the rock next to him and put his head in his hands.

I wanted to rush to his side and hug him and tell him it was okay, but it wasn't in the slightest. He was leaving. Forever.

"Will I ever see you again?" I whispered, my throat dry.

Thick tears built behind my eyes, but I refused to let them escape.

"I don't know. Not for a while. Once I'm installed as king, I will try and come back and see you, but that might not be for some time," he said.

I stared the pebbly sidewalk. I knew that "not for some time" in Créatúir land would mean years in regular time. Since their time moves much slower, a long time to them means an eternity to us. I could be married, with kids, old, even ... dead by the time he came back for me. That was not exactly a nice thought.

"No," I said loudly. Slade raised his head. "No. That's not cool with me. You go, become king or whatever it is you need to do, and then come back to see me as quickly as you can. We'll figure something out—we always have."

He started to shake his head and I stepped closer to him. "I said, no. This is how it's going to be. Got it?" I put my hands on my hips like a little kid demanding candy.

But this wasn't something I could demand.

He stood up and placed a hand on my cheek, eyes still soft. They turned from light violet to a darker purple. "I promise you this—I will come back to see you."

"Soon. You will come back to see me soon," I said quickly and nodded, as though to end the discussion.

He half-smiled and bent down to kiss me, but his lips only lightly brushed mine before he disappeared, shifting into a fog and then back to the Other Realm.

And all I was left with was a light purple mist, an annoyed bodyguard, and a broken heart.

————————

That night, I dreamt about her once again.

I knelt in front of an altar, my white robes pooling around my knees like water. Brilliant gold swirls glinted on either side of the altar and looming statues carved into marble silently watched over my prayers. The center of the room was tall, with an opening at the top. Against the brilliant blue sky, I saw the outline of the Pharos Lighthouse.

I was in the Temple of Isis.

I placed a dish of honey on the marble platform and closed my eyes. I murmured something in Egyptian, some request that Isis take this sacrifice and accept it as worthy. I said my prayers, asking Isis to watch over my children and my kingdom, over and over again until the words were just sounds—like a low hum.

I felt a warmth move up my legs and to the top of my head, so I opened my eyes. The honey on the altar was gone, replaced with a glowing ball of light. I reached forward and touched it. The white-gold light moved up my finger and spread through my whole body. It moved down my white robes, which flashed and glowed.

The power coursed through my blood, pumping and shimmering. I expected it to settle down, like a wave crashing against a beach. But it didn't. It stayed, and became mine to keep.

My fingers shaking, I touched a small scratch on my foot where a sharp stone had scraped me. It instantly healed, the skin coming back to life and regenerating.

"My queen?" said a voice behind me.

I turned around and there stood Aquinias, the scribe with the tattoo. "She has found favor with me," I said. I held up my fingertip, which faintly glowed.

He bowed his head and glanced at the carvings on the inside of the temple, his eyes resting on one in particular that had gold and blue ankhs reaching up toward the sky. "You have secured your future. I will pray to the gods for your safe return."

SIXTEEN

Pepperoni? Gross," Morgana muttered as she held up a limp piece of pizza. It wilted in her hand, cheese ready to slide off onto the floor.

"Sorry, I wasn't sure what you all liked, so I just got a bunch of different kinds." Declan shifted uncomfortably under Morgana's stare. She was wearing a long black robe with blue feathers ringing the bottom, and her headpiece had a jewel that came down over the center of her forehead. At least she'd kept her pointy hat and broom at home.

"She's fine," I said with a dismissive hand wave. I pointed to another box. "There's vegetarian over there if you're going to be high maintenance."

Morgana grumbled and walked around the table. My sisters had come over for dinner—pizza night, which Luther first called a "pizza party" until I reminded him that none of us were ten years old and unless said "party" included gift bags and a piñata, calling it "dinner" was fine.

"Don't you get lonely here?" Gia whispered as she rested her head on my shoulder.

I smiled and shrugged. "I'm fine," I said quickly, then took a huge bite of pepper and onion pizza, hoping my sisters would think my eyes were watering due to the spices. It had been the longest seven days of my life.

"It must be nice not to have to do any chores," Leah offered as she picked at a slice of cheese. She flicked her finger over the crust. "We had to clean the garage out yesterday." She eyed Zombo lying at her feet and wrinkled her nose. I'd given up on trying to send him back to . . . wherever he came from. He had become my buddy—my only source of daily affection—even if his fur was kind of falling off.

I nodded. "It's great. Have fun doing slave labor for Mom and Dad." I swallowed quickly as I thought of my soft purple comforter at home and the way my dad laughed at those dumb funny-home-video shows. I thought of my friends, of parties, of being . . . normal. For so long I'd wanted a power or a gift like my sisters—in other words, to be "normal" in my family. Now, it seemed, I had one, and suddenly I missed my regular, nonmagical life. Of course, it didn't help that I was stuck in an office compound with a bunch of guys who didn't seem interested in having an actual conversation with me.

"Can I get anyone anything? More napkins?" Declan inched toward the door.

"No. Stay!" Gia said. "We want to know more about the person our sister is spending time with."

Declan turned red and I quickly said, "We're not spending time together." Declan shifted uncomfortably and glanced at me.

Oh no. Not him, too.

Really?

I felt a bead of sweat start to move down my back as I considered the possibility that Declan might have a crush on me.

"Do you have a girlfriend?" Morgana asked him, her eyes narrowed.

Declan turned a deeper shade of red and I put my head in my hands. I was beyond relived when I heard him say, "Yes. Back at school. Hannah." He quickly hurried out of the room before my sisters could interrogate him further. Morgana would probably give him some love potion to increase his spiritual connection to Hannah.

I looked down at the bracelet on my right hand, the pearl and onyx braided cuff that Slade had given me last year. "How—how is Slade?" I quietly asked Leah as I grabbed another piece of pizza.

Leah looked at me and said, "He's good. He took the throne yesterday."

I nodded and clamped my teeth together to keep my

chin from wobbling. I remembered my mom telling me on the phone that Leah was at a Créatúir function, but I never stopped to consider that it could be Slade's coronation. "Awesome. Good for him." I bit the inside of my mouth, hard enough to draw blood, and forced myself to take another huge bite of food.

I will see him again. I will see him again when this is all done. This is just temporary.

The night before, Curt had briefed me about the progress the Order was making regarding the Book's precise location. I couldn't imagine it would take that much longer to find it, take it, and deliver it to me to destroy. Declan was so pleased by the update that he said I only had to study Egyptian history for a few more days before we could move on to details about Isis and her powers.

Morgana reached across the table and put her hand over mine. "I can't imagine how hard this is for you. I'm so sorry you're going through this, but we're all here for you. And it will get better soon. Promise."

I flashed a quick, hard smile. "Thanks," I said quickly before pulling my hand away. "I know."

Declan cleared his throat from the doorway. "Looks like you need some more plates," he said before he ran away again. We could practically see the tracks of fire that he made as he ran down the hallway.

I could feel my sisters all staring at me as I slowly took

a long sip of water. "What?" I finally said, slamming the water bottle down. Liquid went all over the table.

"He's cute," Gia said with a small laugh.

"Ew. He hates me. Gross. Stop. Please," I said, rolling my eyes. I scrunched my face up and made a horrible face, as though that would make everyone shut up.

"Well, at least you have a good-looking guy to protect you. It would be a bummer if all the guys were old and ugly," Gia said.

"I guess..." I started to say when I heard yelling outside the conference room. My heart started to pound and my eyes grew wide. "Stay here. Don't do anything." I started to rise from my chair.

They're here. The Octavians are here.

"Call 911! We have to get him to the hospital!" I heard Declan scream as the shuffles grew closer. He and Luther appeared, half-carrying, half-dragging Curt, who was bleeding all over the carpet. His eyes were half-shut and his face was gray and ashen.

"What happened?" I screeched. Declan knelt down next to Curt and put a hand on his neck, the source of the blood. It had been hard to tell at first, since his entire body was soaked.

"911!" Declan screamed again.

"On it!" Morgana said from behind me. I heard Gia and Leah whimper but I didn't turn back.

"What happened?" I said again. I stood over Declan and

watched as he pressed his hand into Curt's neck, but blood just kept pouring out like from a faucet.

Curt moaned and Declan said, "Stay with me. Stay with me." But we all knew that wasn't going to happen, not with the rivers of blood everywhere. There was one final shudder and then Curt's body went limp. Declan closed Curt's eyes and slowly lowered him to the floor.

I closed my eyes and wished with all my might that I could bring him back, like I'd done with Zombo. I tried to summon that feral instinct I'd felt in the Kerry Piper with Slade, but I couldn't get the floodgates to open. They just bubbled below the surface.

"The Octavians got to him," Declan said quietly, as he stood up and stared at the blood on his hands. I looked down at Curt's neck and saw a neatly cut-out square of skin.

They had cut the tattoo off his neck.

"I found him outside. It was two Octavians. I fired at them and they ran away," Luther said. It was then that I noticed the glint of a gun in his hand.

"How could he—they?" Declan whispered to the floor.

"He?" I asked, but Declan didn't answer. He put his head in his hands.

Morgana reached forward and pulled me toward her. I closed my eyes and buried my face in my oldest sister's shoulder. I felt Gia and Leah come up behind me and form a protective circle, squeezing me tight in between them.

Yet despite the collective power of my extraordinary

sisters, the message from the Octavians was clear: *Give her to us.*

My sisters circled around me tighter as if to say: *Never.*

SEVENTEEN

The tiny private plane dipped again, and I clutched the sides of my seat. "I feel like I'm on a plane made of Legos," I grumbled. I looked over at Declan, who was purposefully staring out the window, probably praying that I would suddenly develop laryngitis.

We'd left at the crack of dawn. John and Luther had spent the night making frantic phone calls and hurrying back and forth between their offices, waving papers around and snapping at each other. I'd dozed in the conference room, my sisters all around me, under the watchful eye of Declan. Then John came in and told us that arrangements had been made to fly to another of the Order's offices for protection. There'd been no people anywhere at the small airport when we'd departed, which wasn't very reassuring.

I sighed loudly and snuck another glance at Declan. "Is this plane even safe for—" I began, and he finally looked at me.

"I heard you. There's nothing we can do about it. This was the only plane available on such short notice, so deal with it," he snapped, then turned his face back to the window.

I studied his face and, for the first time, realized that he was grieving. In the bloody aftermath and confusion after Curt died in the Order's headquarters, I never stopped to consider how his death might affect the remaining members. I never stopped to wonder whether Declan was mourning the loss of a coworker and friend.

"I'm sorry about Curt," I said quietly to the window. I couldn't see anything but black sky and the occasional raindrop hitting the glass.

"Thanks," Declan said. He shifted in his chair and rested his head against the window, eyes closed.

I knew I should probably do the same, but adrenaline was still pumping through my veins. The Octavians obviously knew where we were, and how to get to us. As much as I hated being a fugitive, I knew we had to go on the run. I liked being alive, thankyouverymuch.

The Order wouldn't tell my parents or my sisters or even me where we were going, lest one of the Octavians get to them first. And everyone assured me that my family would be safe as long as I was far away. My sisters said some protection spells, and Morgana slipped some quartz into my pocket for extra insurance as we left the compound.

I'd boarded the plane clutching my lavender pillow, from my bed at home, like a kid going on her first road trip. Declan and Luther grunted at an open seat and I sat, biting back tears. I steadied my breath as I realized it was just me—no family, no friends, no Slade. I was alone, on a tiny airplane, being taken to some random location because of something I couldn't control or understand and didn't ask for.

Sure, I was with people who cared about my survival, but only because of what I could do for them, or what kind of power I might have. If I wasn't the reincarnation of Cleopatra, they wouldn't care if I was alive or dead.

I closed my eyes tightly, tried to clear my mind, and wished for sleep. It wasn't too hard, since I drifted off quickly.

Too quickly. Suspiciously fast.

The last thing I thought before passing out was how much I wanted a night where I wasn't afraid that she would haunt my dreams.

―――――

I heard the commotion of the plane landing and tried to pry my eyes open, but sleep still held on to me. The voices sounded far away, and I wanted them to stay that way. I was about to drift off again when I felt someone shake my shoulders.

"Rhea. Rhea, wake up," Declan said.

I batted at my face and slowly opened my eyes, my vision blurred. I felt like I'd taken about fifty sleeping pills. "What happened?" I slurred, not fully in control of my mouth.

Declan kneeled in front of me. "I'm sorry. John insisted. We gave you something to help you sleep."

"You did what?" I tried to shriek, but it came out slurred and weak and I drooled all over my chin.

"We thought you needed some rest. You hadn't been sleeping well and we were worried," Declan said. He handed me a Kleenex and helped me struggle to my feet.

"I can't believe you did that. You guys are a bunch of jerks," I mumbled as I stepped toward the exit. I shook my head and the cobwebs cleared slightly. I didn't know what it felt like to be drunk, but I was sure this feeling was pretty close.

I stepped off the plane and the heat immediately blasted my face, even in the darkness. I squinted down at the tiny runway and couldn't see anything—not even a speck of light—for miles.

"Where are we?" I asked Declan as he started down the stairs in front of me, glancing back up to make sure I didn't tumble. I slowly, methodically, went down one stair at a time.

"Don't you know?" His voice was quiet, somber.

"Clearly, no." We definitely were somewhere south, since it was much too warm to be summer anywhere near Westerville.

Wait, is that … sand?

"Please tell me we're not where I think we are," I said. I stopped at the end of the staircase and laboriously folded my arms across my chest.

Declan sighed, then stopped and turned around. The look on his face told me I was right.

"You—you brought me to—" I couldn't even finish the sentence.

"Egypt," Luther said from behind me as he elbowed me out of his way with a huge black bag over his shoulder.

"Why the hell are we *here*?" I shouted. I threw my lavender pillow down on the runway for emphasis. "You drugged me and took me out of the *country*? Kidnappers!" I shrieked. Sleeping pills or not, I spun around, ready to run back onto the plane and tell the pilot to hightail it straight out of the old country. I'd seriously thought we were just going to another part of the U.S.—one with a beach, hopefully—and not halfway around the world. Sure, the flight was long, but since I'd fallen asleep I had no concept of how long we were actually in the air.

"It was the only logical choice. This is where our main headquarters are. You will have all the resources and training you need at your disposal," Declan said. "This is the only place where we can keep you safe." He shook his head and started to turn his back on me.

"No. Take me home." There was no way I was spending who-knows-how-long in this country where I would probably roast to death and die next to a sphinx at the hands of the Octavians. I may have inherited Cleopatra's spirit, but I definitely did not inherit her darker complexion. Nope, I was stuck with my fair Irish skin, which always reacted to the sun like a bad report card burning in the fireplace, curling up at the edges. My head was already steaming and it was only nighttime.

"Sure, go ahead. Go back home and see how quickly the Octavians come for you and your sisters," Declan said. His back was still turned, but he glanced back and met my eyes. Then he looked at my neck. "And maybe they'll let your sisters stay alive ... or maybe not."

A shiver ran down my spine as I thought of my family—so far away. But safe.

"This is ridiculous," I muttered as I brushed past Declan and headed toward the car where Luther and John were loading our bags. Even though I'd only walked about twenty feet, I was already sweating profusely. "Awesome," I thought as I realized I'd packed mostly jeans, long-sleeved shirts, and a windbreaker.

I always thought my first trip out of the U.S. would

be my honeymoon, or maybe a jaunt to Mexico for spring break during college.

I never expected it to be just me, three cranky guys, and a bunch of sand.

Snow White and the three stooges, I thought to myself as the car began to pull away from the landing strip.

———————

I expected another office building, maybe this time with an updated copier or a few new tools or something to signify this as the Head Office. And it definitely looked that way from the outside as we pulled up to a square, simple, white brick building. There didn't seem to be any other buildings around, although it was hard to tell in the dark. There were no streetlamps—the only light anywhere was a small fluorescent glow coming from a window near the building's front door. It was silent outside; even the wind seemed to pause.

Declan lead me through a small, barren lobby into an elevator and pressed "B4." We got off the elevator and I was struck speechless.

The ceiling soared at least thirty feet high, and the walls were carved and painted with intricate hieroglyphs. Gold leaf, brilliant blues, and fire reds swirled together on the drawings. I recognized several of them—the eye of Horus,

Osiris and Isis and Ra. There were giant, sparkly cranes as large as humans guarding the doors to what looked like a temple. On the ceiling was a giant image of Isis. Her golden body knelt on the ground and her arms were outstretched; brilliantly colored feathers radiated from her arms like sunbeams. On her head was the crown of Hathor: two horns with a solar disk in between them.

I studied her face, and her dark eyes seemed to glint at me. Then I noticed that underneath Isis was a rendering of the same eye tattoo that Declan and his friends had.

"This place is amazing," I said in a whisper.

"It's been around for centuries," Declan said simply, with a shrug. Clearly, all the gold leaf in the world didn't impress him the same way as it did me. "We fund ourselves by selling off small portions of artifacts—antiquities which have been in our possession for years—that Mark Antony collected during his conquests of eastern Europe."

"Holy crap," I said as I followed Declan down the hallway toward a brilliant purple door. I shivered … it felt like all the hieroglyphs on the walls were looking at me, like those creepy porcelain dolls with the eyes that follow you everywhere.

Declan pushed open the door. Standing in the room was a group of people—mostly men, but a few burly-looking women as well. They all looked like they'd been pulled from their beds in the middle of the night. Which, considering the time, was most likely the case.

Still, despite the late hour and the obvious disruption we were causing, I thought that being at headquarters would at least mean a warm welcome, or a smile, or ... something friendly.

But no.

They all glared at me with the fire of a thousand Egyptian suns. They shook their heads and muttered under their breath.

Jeez. Sorry.

"So this is the girl," said a guy with a long scar on his face. Everyone in the room smirked.

"Excuse—" I started to say, but Declan grabbed my elbow.

"This is Rhea, everyone," John said. "She's going to stay here with us for safety until the Book is out of the hands of the Octavians." Everyone in the room grumbled but nodded.

"Why is he here?" A member of the Order glared at Declan. He and John shared a long look—a standoff—as my head snapped back and forth between them.

"He's a valued member of our organization, that's why," John finally said.

"What was that all about?" I asked as Declan walked me to my room.

"Look." Declan stopped abruptly in the hallway. "It's really not a big deal, but I also have a connection to the Octavians."

I took a step back from him and crossed my arms over my chest. "What do you mean?" I eyed the door—my escape route should I need to run.

"My uncle, who raised me, is involved with them. He actually raised me in their organization, telling me my parents were Octavians, but they were really on the other side." He swallowed hard and cleared his throat. "When I found out, I defected to the Order—to the *right* side. To this side."

I took a deep breath and relaxed my stance. "I'm sorry. That must be awful to be on the opposite side from your family." My sisters and I had always been on the same side in everything that mattered. I couldn't imagine having to face off against someone I loved.

"It's fine." Declan shrugged and kept walking down the hallway. He stopped in front of a white door. "Look, if you feel unwelcome here, it's because you are. You being here means that they're all in danger. Yes, Cleopatra was a great queen, but she wasn't always loved. She hurt a lot of people for her own purposes and a lot of people died trying to protect her. Nobody wants to see that happen again."

"Well, me neither. I don't want to be here either. Did you tell them that?" I said over my shoulder as I stepped into my room. I half-expected/half-hoped that it would be as ornately decorated as the hallways, but it was a basic room with a white bed, dresser, and lamp. The rest of the head-quarters might be fit for a queen, but they were sending a clear message to me with the room: you might be special, but don't act like it.

"Just get settled in and then come and find me. Now that you're here, we have some work to do," Declan said.

"Work?" I threw my bag down on my bed and flopped onto it.

"Here in Egypt there are a lot of artifacts from the ancient kingdom and Cleopatra's time. Tomorrow, you'll meet with a tutor and begin to study some of the archived documents such as carved prayers to Isis uncovered from temple walls. Now that we're here, we can work more intensively on access-ing your powers."

"Accessing? What if I become stressed out and acciden-tally raise something... undead?" I whispered.

"That's the point. You need to learn to control your stress reactions. Control *yourself*. Tone it down so you don't bring up some corpse minding its own business."

Tone it down. Control yourself. This was beginning to sound like one of my mom's lectures.

Before I could respond, Declan yawned. "It's late ... early... whatever. You need to sleep so you can concentrate in the morning." I nodded and began to follow him down the hallway toward a row of bedrooms. "Just try not to reanimate anything tonight, okay?" he added. "I need a decent night of sleep."

I rolled my eyes. "*Now* you start cracking jokes."

EIGHTEEN

I fell asleep hard, the sleeping pills still in my system. I think I was just about to start dreaming when I heard a voice.

"Rhea. Rhea, wake up."

I felt a hand on my shoulder and a light shake.

They're here. They found me.

I tried to sit up in bed and scream, but a hand clapped over my mouth.

This is it. I'm dead. Or worse.

"It's just me," Slade whispered into my ear.

My body relaxed and I exhaled loudly as he removed his hand from my face. I whirled around and threw my arms around his neck. "What are you doing here?" I said, my eyes tightly shut.

"I had to see you," he said. I leaned back and squinted at his frame in the darkness. His body was just a shadow, but his eyes were a softly glowing purple—a sight that would definitely unnerve most regular girls, but more comforting than just about anything I'd ever seen.

I threw my arms around him again and buried my face in his shoulder. He smelled like burning firewood. "I thought you couldn't leave the Other Realm for a while."

"I slipped away during the Summer Festival," he whispered.

"Oh." I had learned about the event from Leah, who was no doubt there right now. She told me it was a few days of celebration, culminating in parades, feasts, and a flotilla of boats all decorated with fairy lights. She also said it was sort of their version of spring break, and there was all kinds of bad behavior thanks to the honeyed wine.

"Leah's covering for me," he said, reading my mind.

Maybe it was the mention of my sister, or maybe it was having him here in front of me, real and breathing, but I suddenly slumped forward, put my face in my hands, and started to sob. Nothing made sense any more. I was essentially a prisoner—and even though everyone kept telling me it was for my own good, that there was a purpose, I still felt like I'd been sent away to juvie without so much as a trial. And the Order in Egypt certainly hadn't welcomed me with open arms.

Slade pulled my face toward him and kissed me lightly.

I took a deep breath and quickly wiped my eyes. "How did you know where to find me?" I asked.

He smiled and I could see him shaking his head, even in the darkness of my room. "You always forget that I can be anywhere, at any time."

"Oh, right. Human hazard, I guess." I tried to laugh, but it sounded hollow and empty as it bounced around the room and fizzled like a dying firecracker. "So, how long can you stay?" I asked the question but I knew the answer.

"Not long. Just another minute or so before they realize I'm gone. I'm the Dark King, after all, so my absence is somewhat obvious if I'm missing for too long. I need to head back soon for the reenactment of the Battle of Thothmore." He put his hand on my knee and I laced my fingers through his.

Why did everything in my life always have to be so ridiculously complicated? Why couldn't I just have fallen for a normal guy who didn't have to shapeshift back to his realm? Why couldn't I have been born as the reincarnation of some boring, anonymous person? Someone different, anyone different. Or at least someone who didn't have centuries of bad blood behind her and a bunch of guys who wanted to kill her or kidnap her or use her for their own purposes.

I would even have settled for being reincarnated as my sister's cat.

"Don't—" I started to say, when my bedroom door

swung open. Light flooded the room and I squinted at the dark figure in the doorway.

"Who's in here with you?" Declan called.

I stood up, hand shielding my face from the light in the hallway. "It's okay. It's just Slade."

Declan flipped on the overhead light and stood there, his eyes narrowed. He was wearing light blue pajama bottoms and no shirt. It was a little awkward, standing there in my room with my boyfriend and another half-naked guy.

My mother would so ground me right now.

"This is a secure facility. How did you . . ." Declan trailed off. He looked at Slade and nodded. "Right. I forgot."

"I was just leaving," Slade said. He shot Declan a dirty look, his eyes shifting to black and then back to purple. Declan shrank back a little and cleared his throat.

"Now?" I squeaked. Was he really going to make me say goodbye like this, in front of Declan?

"I have to," he said simply. He pulled my elbows toward him and put my arms around his waist.

"When will I see you again?" I whispered into his shirt.

"I don't know. I'll try to get away again soon, but remember how time passes there. A week to you is only a day to us." He bent down and kissed me, a kiss I never wanted to end . . . except for when I heard Declan loudly clear his throat in the doorway.

"Take a picture," I muttered to him as Slade and I broke apart.

Slade reached up and gently put his palm on my cheek. I started to close my eyes, but then he was gone.

A heavy ache ripped through my chest as I realized I was so sick—so very, very sick—of saying goodbye.

"Are you all right?" Declan asked quietly.

"I'm fine." I turned toward my bed and sat down, my back to him.

"I know how much it sucks to miss someone," he said.

I thought of his girlfriend, Hannah, and nodded. "Thanks. Shut the light out when you leave, please."

I heard him hesitate, but then the lights shut off and the door closed.

And it was dark once more.

———————

That night, I dreamt of snakes. Of snakes swallowing me whole, gnawing at my face, and sinking their fangs into my arms. I could feel their poison course through my veins, burning me from the inside out like a white-hot fire.

I dreamt of my sisters, of snakes ripping at them, crushing them and poisoning them while I watched. Gia, Morgana, and Leah all lay at my feet, gasping for breath but I couldn't help them. A red and black snake was crushing my windpipe and I couldn't even scream. All I could do was watch them die.

I woke up, sobs racking through my chest as I gasped

for air. I balled my fists up and pressed them into my eyes, and then I could finally scream.

I screamed a scream that let out all of my frustration at being cooped up in two different places—of being separated from my friends, my family, my boyfriend.

I screamed a scream that could wake the dead.

Literally.

As my scream ended, I was suddenly aware of a real hissing sound at the end of the bed. It kind of sounded like a burst water pipe or a steam shower gone awry, but my blood ran cold and I started to sweat.

Sssssssssss

It started to come closer and I didn't move.

I'm imagining this. I'm still dreaming.

Ssssssss

It was all around me, creeping toward my arm. I jumped up and flicked on the light—and stared at my bed.

On it was a decaying, gray and black snake. Its scales were falling off and its white-blue glassy eyes stared at me. It opened its mouth and hissed, its rotting yellow fangs still very much in business. On the floor next to my bed was a crack in the floor; dirt mounds littered the carpet.

I'd summoned a snake. A very-much dead one.

"Help!" I screamed as I backed against the door, wishing Zombo was there. John had made me leave him behind in Westerville. Zombo whined, but my sisters had promised to take good care of him and not drop him off at the nearest mortuary.

I pitched forward as the door opened behind me, but I fell to the side, away from the snake.

"What the hell is that?" Luther yelled, pointing at my bed.

"I don't know! Haven't you ever seen a zombie snake before?" I shrieked as I crawled away on the floor. "Kill it or something!"

"How?" Luther picked up my alarm clock and tried to hit the snake, but it slithered out of the way and stared at me. "How in the world did you do this?"

"I have no idea!"

"Well, send it back!"

I balled up my fists and closed my eyes and screamed again, this time for the creature to return to its grave in the dirt where it was nice and warm and cozy—but no dice. In fact, it only seemed to grow bigger.

"Stay back!" John said from the doorway. He had a hammer in his hand. I closed my eyes as I heard a sickening crunch and splat. "It's dead. Again."

I slowly opened one eye and saw zombie snake-body parts all over my bed. Sweet dreams to me.

"How did she do it?" Luther asked John quietly.

John considered the hammer in his hands, which was covered in black snake blood. "I don't know. She's done it once before, but she's not supposed to be able to do it without the Book."

"Well, she better get it under control before we all wind up dead," Luther snapped, slamming the door behind him.

I stared at John, my palms in the air. "So now it's my fault?"

"Tomorrow morning. You will pay attention in your training tomorrow morning. Or he's right: we *will* all end up dead." John clicked the door shut behind him, and I stared at my mess of a bed.

NINETEEN

The symbols on the paper in front of me seemed to stare back at me, taunting me with their wavy lines and swoops. "I feel like I'm never going to be able to memorize the hieroglyphic alphabet," I moaned, resting my head against the wooden table in the library's study room.

"I know. I'm sorry." My tutor, Mary, gave me a sympathetic look. Her short, bleached-blond hair stuck out in every direction, giving her appearance of having been electrocuted.

I looked up and gave her the most pathetic look I could muster. As one of the few female members of the Order, she understood how draining it was being around guys who were too focused on retrieving ancient artifacts to actually, on occasion, have a real conversation about … the weather. Sports.

Anything.

It was only my first day in Egypt and already I was already starting to feel like a very-well-treated hostage. I'd woken up to a man with a white beard delivering breakfast to me. It was a muffin with some Greek yogurt. I'd tried to joke that the yogurt was particularly appropriate since Cleopatra was actually Greek, but he didn't laugh. It seemed like no one around here laughed.

After my quick breakfast, Declan came to get me and brought me to the library. Dark paneled walls and two floating staircases framed a long wooden table where I was supposed to study each day with Mary until we had Cleopatra's Book of the Dead in our possession. I didn't even get to leave for lunch—another grumpy Order member brought a few peanut butter and jelly sandwiches to the library, and Mary forced me to speak to her in ancient Egyptian while we ate. I assumed there would be more Egyptian at dinnertime.

I'd spent so much of the day in silence that I think I had already memorized the exact angle of each of Mary's blond spikes.

I sighed and looked down at the signs and translations in front of me. Mary had said I needed to finish learning hieroglyphs first, and then we would move on to meditative techniques designed to control my stress reactions so I wouldn't inadvertently summon anything that should stay underground. When we finally got the Book, all of this training would help me immediately identify which spell would destroy the Book, and then perform it as quickly as possible.

I studied my tutor for a minute and realized I had no idea where they were all going to go, or what they would do, once the Book was destroyed. I didn't know if they had homes of their own. I hoped they all had lives tucked away somewhere, in some corner of the world, just like I did.

"So," Mary started to say, "if you'll just turn the page and—"

I cut her off. "Are you married?"

Mary sat back and shook her head. "No. Being here makes it a little difficult to actually have a social life." Sadness flashed in her bright green eyes.

"Oh. Sorry. Can't you just leave?" I said.

She gave me a withering look and her spikes seemed pointier. "It's my job, so not really. After all this is over, I plan on going back to my museum and continuing my boring life collecting and cataloguing pieces." She surveyed me critically. "When I signed up for this gig years ago, I never thought she would actually be born within my lifetime."

"Oh. Sorry," I said. I felt guilty until I realized that *I* didn't sign up for this "gig" either.

"So, back to the exact translation of the—"

I collapsed forward on the table in a heap.

"Please. No. Let's go outside. Do something. Anything, before I try to burn this entire building down."

Mary looked startled, and I realized she wasn't quite used to my dramatic statements.

"You know what I mean. Not literally." I waved my hand around. She started to shake her head, but I reached forward and grabbed her hand. "Please."

Her eyes flickered with excitement, and I realized that she was just as desperate to leave as me.

Twenty minutes later, I was squished in the back of a white Land Rover, in between Mary and Luther, with Declan sitting shotgun and John driving. When I'd demanded to be let outside for just ten minutes, to go somewhere, anywhere, they'd quickly refused—but I reminded them I was there voluntarily and could leave whenever I wanted. They reluctantly agreed to allow me to go food shopping with them at the market.

I craned my neck and inhaled sharply as I took in the landscape around us. For miles and miles behind us, all I could see was sand. It ran along either side of our car like a never ending beach. As we approached the city, I could see tall modern buildings.

"The Mediterranean is just beyond those buildings," Mary murmured.

I squinted my eyes and tried to imagine the world as it looked in Cleopatra's days. In pictures and in my visions the buildings looked like they were made out of hardened sand, like sandcastles. And Declan said the sea level was much lower, since over the past thousands of years there had been earthquakes and natural disasters that caused almost everything from Cleopatra's time to crumble into the sea.

Maybe they should've been left alone, to disintegrate like everything else in the natural world. Instead, we were dredging up the past, literally and figuratively.

Yeah, but I didn't choose this, I reminded myself, a thought that brought me no comfort.

John pulled the car through the crowded streets. "Put this on," Mary said as she threw a black sheetlike garment over my head. "It's a burka—a custom among many women here—and it's just the thing to keep you hidden if any of Octavians are around." She put one over her own head, but it jutted out at weird angles thanks to her hair. I noticed it had an ankh on it—the Order's symbol for Cleopatra. She was acting as a decoy, like when celebrities try to leave nightclubs and don't want the paparazzi to capture them stumbling down the sidewalk.

"Ten minutes," John barked as we parked next to an open-air market. "We're staying for ten minutes, just long enough to pick up dinner for everyone, and then we're going back to the compound."

I stepped out of the car, struggling to see through the eye slits in the black material. The first thing I felt was the slip of the paving stones under my feet and the burning-hot rays of the sun. It was the kind of hot that made me feel like I was pulling a cake out of the oven and couldn't figure out how to move my head away. I immediately felt about a million drips of sweat move down my body.

"Are we actually on the equator right now?" I asked Declan.

"Quiet," he hissed, his eyes scanning the crowd of people walking around and perusing the booths. "Just stay next to me."

"Great," I muttered to myself.

We walked toward the market, a line of bodies. I was flanked by Declan on one side and Luther on the other. Mary and John walked in front of us. I couldn't see very well through the burka, and it felt like people were pushing me all around, grabbing at me in the burning sunlight. My entire body became slicked with sweat, like I'd taken a shower with my clothes on, as I tried to keep up with everyone. I had very little peripheral vision and it felt like I was trapped in a box, slowly being suffocated to death.

I felt a shove from behind and pitched forward. My arms were caught in the fabric and I couldn't put them up in front of me to brace my fall. I rammed into John and knocked him to the ground. I heard scuffling around me and a scream. I tried to put my hands up over my head, but they were pinned down by a heavy arm. I started to kick and thrash but the arm held me down.

The sounds caved in around me, the frantic staccato of a foreign language. Then I heard something I understood:

"The time has almost come."

I looked up and saw four Octavians standing above us—some of the same men who had attacked me at the Kerry Piper. They were huge, the size of NFL linebackers.

"Not being so careful after all, we see," one of them said. I saw the glint of a bloody knife in his hand.

Mary lay at their feet, clutching her forearm as drops of blood fell into the sand. Luther was pressing his hand against her skin, trying to stop the bleeding. I then realized it was Declan who'd pinned me down on the ground, his arm over me protectively.

The four of them stepped toward Declan and me. He tightened his grip. They stared down at me and I saw one raise the knife. I held my breath as I realized I was about to die.

I closed my eyes and thought of my sisters.

Of Slade.

Of my parents.

The Octavian sheathed his knife and laughed. He looked me straight in the eyes and said, "My queen." Then he and his three friends disappeared into the crowd.

I didn't understand why they didn't kill or kidnap me. But then I remembered Slade's story about how the Créatúir grow pomegranates every year. There are always a few Créatúir who want to pick the pomegranates early, and end up being disappointed because they grabbed them before they were ready—before the fruits were ripe and prime.

The ones who waited until they were just right truly got to enjoy what the pomegranate was capable of.

I was here, in Egypt. Being trained in Ancient Egyptian culture, language, and mythology.

If they took me now, I'd have trouble reading from the Book of the Dead for them.

But if they waited too long—waited until I was strong enough to defend myself and to fight back—I'd be one hell of a weapon.

TWENTY

O h look. What a cute painting." I pointed to a picture
of half-cat/half-human cutting the head off a servant
kneeling in front of him. Blood was spurting everywhere,
and there were regular cats lying around lapping it up.
Behind the dead servant was a line of victims, each waiting
his turn to be beheaded.

"The Egyptians were known for their black and white
worldview: life and death, day and night. The whole life process—they didn't shy away from any of it." Declan shrugged
and tried to look serious, but I saw a faint glint in his clear
eyes.

"Clearly. Maybe I'll make this the front of my Christ-
mas card this year." I sighed and pushed the book further
away from me on the table. Ever since the incident in the

marketplace, Mary had, er, taken some time off. She was physically fine, but I'm fairly certain she'd hightailed it out of here calling me the devil under her breath—not that it's something I hadn't heard before from Leah. But because Mary left, Declan was stuck once again educating me on all things Egyptian. He was my new warden, and I now ate my peanut butter and jelly sandwiches each day with him.

He pulled a hefty, somber-looking book out of his bag. "I got this from the Alexandrian Library yesterday. It has a few things I think you need to see." He flipped through it and stopped on the photograph of scroll, which spread across both pages.

I leaned forward and my heart began to beat quickly. "What the ... " It depicted a battle scene. The sky was nearly black, and streaked with purple and gold arrows. There were people in white robes, wearing gold headdresses with big ankhs in the center, fighting with black and green monsters whose limbs were falling off and whose teeth had blood-stains. On the edge of the battle, a few of the monsters were hunched over dead bodies.

Eating them.

"The undead," I whispered, my eyes wide. Declan nodded and sat back in his chair, his fingers laced behind his head. "What is this? Did this happen in the past?" I asked.

Declan shook his head. "No. It hasn't happened ... yet." I remained silent, a sinking feeling growing over my shoulders. "This has been called a prophecy. Look, Cleopatra was gifted with the power to bring the dead back to life, thanks to her connection with Isis. But she was more interested in ruling Egypt, and using her many talents to help the Egyptian people avoid Roman rule. She wasn't about to raise the undead to launch a full-scale war on her enemies—that sort of thing would have been way too risky, since the undead might have destroyed her own people as well."

There was a pause as I considered the picture again and thought of the Octavians. "But *they* will."

Declan's silence confirmed my statement.

My chest felt hot and my ears grew prickly as I spoke slowly. "So, wait. You're telling me that the Octavians want to use me to raise a bunch of undead so they can conquer the world?" Just hearing it said out loud made me start to shake with laughter. "Seriously?" I couldn't help myself. I threw my head back and started roaring until I felt a squeeze on my wrist. "What?" I said as I shook Declan's hand away.

"Everyone will die if this happens. Your sisters, your parents. Me. All of us. Everyone. It's in the prophecy," Declan said. "It's what the Octavians wanted Cleopatra for originally, way back in 30 BC, but she killed herself instead of allowing that to happen."

I stopped laughing. "What does this prophecy say, exactly?"

Declan flipped the book to the back and pointed to a photograph of a tablet. "Can you read this?" I shook my head. "It says, *She will rise again, and this time will call armies from the Underworld to do battle in the natural world.*

The living will fall under the rule of those who command the army of the undead. All of mankind will be ruled by those who rule her."

I swallowed hard. "So I would be their little pet, their weapon, as they take over the world?"

Declan nodded and slowly closed the book. "Now you see what we're fighting against."

I pressed my palms against the table. "If it's in the prophecy, does that mean it's definitely going to happen? Like, do these tablets always come true?"

Declan wouldn't meet my eyes, and I saw a pained expression on his face. After a few long moments, he finally spoke. "They've all come true in the past."

"Queen of the Undead." I tried to muster a laugh, but it got caught in my throat.

Everyone I know will die, and it will be all my fault.

"What if I refuse to help them? Like, what if I just don't raise the dead?" I said. *They can't make me do anything—just ask my parents.* My mother always called me her "selectively deaf child," since every time she called up to our rooms to ask for help with dinner or chores, I would always pretend I didn't hear so that my sisters could get a head start.

Declan shook his head slowly. "Then they will torture you or find ways to make you do what they want. They use your family, your friends, anything." A pained expression flashed on his face and I guessed he was thinking of his uncle, of what his own family member might be capable of doing.

I felt a wave of nausea move up from my stomach, but I swallowed hard and pushed it back down. "So sitting here, in this room, with you—this is going to prevent it all from happening?"

Declan shrugged and leaned forward. "It's the only thing we can do. Our hope is that you can destroy the Book for good."

"So how close are we to finding the Book?" I said, tapping the table.

Declan looked at me before glancing down. "We've pinpointed the Book's exact location."

"Why didn't you tell me this sooner?" I exclaimed.

"Sorry."

I gave him a long look. "I need to meet with everyone and get a status update. Now," I added when he didn't move. He nodded and stood up, and I saw that same hint of a smile on his face.

———

John gave me a withering look before he flipped open his laptop and pressed a few keys. I held my breath as I waited for him to boot everything up. Declan had done what I asked and gathered the key members of the Order together, but they didn't seem to be too happy to stop what they were doing and give me a status update.

My dad used to complain that his captain would call

him into administrative meetings where they'd have to discuss lame things like paperwork instead of being out in public, finding bad guys. But the captain insisted that they needed to "touch base" once in a while, and so everyone on the force was stuck in a conference room for a couple of hours of torture.

I suspected I'd just done the same thing to everyone here. But I didn't care. This was my life—I was the key to preventing the prophecy from coming true. And they better damn well tell me what was going on. No more of this need-to-know basis.

"The location of Cleopatra's tomb is here," John said, pointing to an X on the map near Alexandria. "The Octavians found it in Taposiris Magna, which was an underground cave system that was at the center of the city in 30 BC. The Book was buried in a golden box, in a sarcophagus next to Cleopatra's—her lady-in-waiting's sarcophagus. The ancient Egyptians believed they would need servants in the afterlife, before they returned via reincarnation, and their servants always carried the most valuable artifacts."

I nodded. I knew most of this already. I cleared my throat. "Let's fast-forward a little, to the part where you tell me where the Octavians are hiding the Book."

John gave me a long look before he opened a file folder and took out a photo of a museum with a sphinx sculpture at the entrance. "Here's the museum where they're based. The Book is being kept in an antiquities storage room on the lowest level of the structure. We're meeting later tonight to discuss assembling a team to go in and grab it."

"So this could all be over in a few days?" I tried to keep my voice steady. Once they got the Book, I could destroy it and go home.

"I don't know the exact details, but obviously we're hoping it will happen sooner rather than later," John said. He closed his laptop and faced the room. "Anything else?"

Soon. I could be back home in a couple of days.

I shook my head. John walked out of the room and slammed the door behind him.

I leaned forward and smacked Declan on the forearm "I could be home by the end of the week!" I squeezed his arm in my excitement.

A strange look fell across his face for a moment before he gave me a small smile. "That would be great, but don't get too excited. If it was so easy, we would have it by now, right?"

My face fell a little, but I shook my head. "I'm sure they'll be able to get it."

Declan held my look for a moment before he chuckled. "I'm sure they will too."

"Why are you being like this? Just think—soon I can be with my family and Slade, and you can be with your girlfriend and your family … " I trailed off as I remembered what Declan told me about his uncle being an Octavian.

He gave me a small, sad smile before he walked out the door.

TWENTY-ONE

I lay in my silent room for what felt like hours, thinking I heard footsteps down the hallway, certain they were going to tell me all was A-OK and we had the Book. I tried pacing back and forth, but that made me feel like a mouse that Doppler trapped once on the screened-in porch. I tried counting sheep, counting backwards, and threatening myself with excessive exercise if it didn't fall asleep. Right. Now.

I'm not sure which one did it—maybe the threat of three thousand jumping jacks—but suddenly, I was dreaming.

I was sitting at a glistening white table sparkling with inlaid jewels, with what appeared to be a small board game in front of me. I held up my arms and saw that I was wearing a simple white dress that flowed around my legs. My hair was pulled back and my fingers were free of jewels.

"Your turn, Your Highness." The woman across from me had a youthful face, with wide green eyes and hair that shone like a smooth pane of glass.

I looked down at the board game. It was a rectangle, with different colored squares and playing pieces, and seemed to be a cross between checkers and chess. I glanced around the room. We appeared to be in a bedchamber. From the ornate painting on the walls and ceilings and the jewels dripping from the bedside table, I assumed it was mine.

"Your Highness?" the woman said again. Her brows knitted together and a look of confusion spread across her face.

"Oh! Yes!" I said effortlessly in Egyptian. I poised my hand above the game and tried to will myself to remember how to play. The sides of the board were covered in hieroglyphs, but none of them translated to anything resembling instructions.

"Do you not wish to play Senet anymore?" she asked.

"I think I'm finished," I said quickly. Her face relaxed and she began to pick up the game pieces. I stood up and walked over to the open terrace and stepped outside. My breath caught in my throat at the sight. All of Alexandria spread before me, with its straight, wide roads and white, sun-bleached buildings. I saw people milling about doing business. Huge palm trees ringed the palace where majestic horses were led around. In the distance, the sea sparkled a deep turquoise. A warm wind blew my hair back, rustling my dress, and I smelled vanilla and another scent I couldn't identify, but it tickled the back of my throat.

There was a knock at the door and the woman—who I assumed was a lady-in-waiting—answered the door.

"Your Highness, the High Priestess has a message for you," the lady-in-waiting said.

I nodded my head and beckoned her forward.

"Thank you, Iras," the Priestess said.

Iras. She was one of the ladies-in-waiting who killed themselves with Cleopatra, I thought.

The High Priestess was older than she first appeared. When she was in front of me, I could see lines around her eyes and lips that cracked her dark caramel skin. She wore a white linen tunic and gold sandals.

She glanced at Iras, who was busy packing up the Senet game. "The carvings are in place," she whispered.

I nodded and leaned forward, trying to look as though I knew what she was talking about. Clearly, this was important. "What exactly do they say?"

The High Priestess narrowed her eyes for a moment. "Exactly what you asked. They will be there to guide you upon your return, should the gods allow it." She glanced upward and closed her eyes.

"And how will I know where they are, when I return in the next life?" I whispered.

She opened her eyes. "They are in the most holy of places. Surely the gods will see that it lasts throughout time."

―――――――

"Shhhhh." The whisper tickled my ear as I sat at the desk in my room, reviewing old hieroglyphics charts. Since I couldn't go back to sleep after my dream, I'd decided to study instead of spinning around in my sheets.

I closed my eyes and smiled. "Hey," I said softly. My shoulders slumped forward as I felt a kiss on my neck. I put my hand up and Slade rested his chin it, then turned my palm over and kissed the top of my hand. I turned around and looked up at him. He looked older than I remembered, his face creased a little more, which didn't even make sense since he was a shapeshifter; he could look however he wanted.

This time, though, I didn't ask the dumb question of *So, uh, how did you get in here? There are like guards and stuff.* "How long do you have?" I said instead.

He smiled, his eyes shifting from dark purple to violet. "An hour, to you."

I stood up and threw my arms around his waist and allowed him to press me toward him. If only it could always be like this—if only he could've stayed with me during all of this. If only he hadn't been made king during all of this stuff. I closed my eyes and allowed myself, for the first time in what felt like forever, to feel at home.

I opened my eyes as I heard someone else clear their throat. "Oh hi, Asher." I looked up at Slade questioningly.

Slade snapped his fingers at Asher and he transformed into a mirror image of me. "Just in case anyone comes to check on you."

"Do I really look like that?" I muttered. Asher did look like me, but it was like a weird photocopy where it never looks as good as the original. My hair color was flat, my skin looked sallow, and I definitely was a bit chunkier. But whatever. It was a decoy, and that was all that counted.

I tried not to shiver as I thought of what had happened to my last decoy.

"Ridiculous," Asher muttered. It was me in looks, but he definitely had a guy's voice; I looked like a drag queen. He shuffled over to the bed and lay down, pulling the comforter up to his chin.

Brilliant. If anyone walked in, they would definitely think I was asleep and wouldn't dare disturb me.

"Ready?" Slade asked, palm out.

Of course I was.

———

"It's so beautiful," I said as I took in the landscape. Slade had shifted us to far away in the desert. We sat on a red blanket, with lanterns around us illuminating the darkness. Far off in the distance, I could see the outlines of the pyramids at Giza, and the sphinx. Many of the treasures from ancient times had been destroyed, lost to various ravages of history, but here there was still an eerie sense of being transported back in time. It was the most curious mix of past and present, clashing together. I wondered what events these grains of sand had witnessed. Likely they had seen bloodshed and great monuments crumble into nothing, but I bet they had also seen love and hope and all that fueled people to carry on through tragedy.

I also thought of Cleopatra and what she might have seen, out in the desert with Julius Caesar or Mark Antony. Maybe she stared off at the pyramids too, never realizing how tragically everything would eventually end for her. I imagined she thought her empire would last forever and couldn't fathom that the great monuments Egypt had built would become tourist sites or exhibits in a museum. Artifacts to be viewed for a price.

Despite sharing Cleopatra's mojo, I hoped my ending would be considerably more cheery.

"You seem like you're keeping it together," Slade said as I rested back in his arms. He trailed a finger up my forearm and I shivered.

"I'm trying to. It isn't easy, though. There's no one here to talk to or hang out with. But they said they're going to get the Book soon, so this will all be over soon." My words were confident, but they sounded hollow.

He was silent and I could hear his heart beating through his chest. "After all this is over—after you go home—I'm coming with you."

I sat up and turned around. "What do you mean?"

His eyes glinted and he smiled. "I mean, I'm coming with you. Here. In your world. I'm going to give up the kingship so we can be together."

My eyes grew wide. "No! You can't!" When his brow furrowed, I continued. "Of course, I want you to, but you can't give all that up for me."

Slade shook his head. "It's done. I've made my decision."

A warmth spread through my stomach as I finally, finally saw a light at the end of the Egyptian tunnel. We would have the Book, I would read the destruction spell, and then I could go home with Slade.

It was the most perfect plan I'd ever heard.

I threw my arms around him and wrapped my legs around his waist. "I love you," I said.

He hugged me tight but didn't say anything. It was okay—he was still learning about this world. I knew he loved me right back. He was giving up his kingship for me.

I thought briefly of how the men in Cleopatra's time had given up kingdoms and power for her, but I knew this was different.

"We should go back soon, before Asher starts to wander off," Slade said into my hair.

I nodded but grabbed him even tighter, like I hoped my body would just melt into his and we wouldn't have to be apart at all, even for a short bit. My fingertips started to tingle and I kept my eyes closed through the shift. And then we were back in my bedroom.

Asher was half out of his glamour, sitting up in bed watching the news. It was my hair and body, but his masculine face.

Now I definitely look like a drag queen.

"Finally," he grumped as he got out of bed and shifted back into his regular form. "No offense, but being you kind of sucks."

"Tell me about it," I said. But I couldn't stop smiling. I looked up at Slade.

"Soon," he said. He bent down to kiss me, and then he and Asher vanished into the air. I was left craning my neck upward. But no matter, I would have him back soon.

I will have everything back soon.

I threw myself on my bed and bounced a few times, sighing happily.

I tried to picture my sister's face when she heard the news about Slade. "Leah's going to kill me," I laughed.

Yeah, well, she wouldn't be the first to try.

I spent the rest of the night dreaming of Slade—of being back home, sitting in my room with him, my sisters down the hallway and my parents nearby. I dreamed of Westerville High, of going to the Homecoming dance, of cute shoes and flatirons and long sparkly earrings.

I even dreamed of cuddling with Doppler and laughing when he incorrectly predicted the weather. Again.

I woke up the next morning with a glow still around me, the fuzzy edges of sleep comforting me like a warm blanket.

Everything is going to be okay.

With an incurably dorky smile on my face, I walked out of my room. But I slammed into someone in the hallway. It was my decoy. Well, my former decoy/teacher/stabbing victim.

"OW!" Mary screamed, holding her arm.

"Oh no! I'm so sorry!" I reached forward and gestured toward her arm. Since she'd disappeared from the compound after the attack, I'd figured she was home with her family or maybe reunited with her museum artifacts.

"Yeah, I'm sure you are," she snapped, shrinking back from me. She gingerly inspected the bandage, which was dotted with blood.

"Should I get someone?" I asked as I glanced around. The halls were empty and a look at the clock told me it was five in the morning. I guessed that being out with Slade had stirred up too much adrenaline. I hadn't been up this early since...never.

"I'll be fine." Mary frowned. She looked at me, eyes

hard, in a way that made my stomach drop. Even her pointy bleached-blond hair seemed to glare at me.

She hates me.

"I think you've done enough," she added. She crossed her arms over her chest, her legs spread wide, and raised her eyebrows at me.

She definitely hates me.

"I'm sorry that happened to you," I said. I knew that Mary was probably a really nice person, and I couldn't blame her for thinking I was some sort of curse. I'd often wondered that myself—if my life was worth it. Worth all of this. "I'm sorry this happened to any of us," I added, thinking of Curt's bleeding neck. "I never wanted any of this."

Regardless of what I might want, it didn't matter. At least it would all soon be over.

Her face softened for a moment and she cocked her head slightly to the side, sizing me up and down in a way that made me shift uncomfortably. Then she smiled gently and stepped toward me, her hand on my face. "I'm going to tell you something."

"What?" I said shakily, my heart in my throat. Her oddly calm demeanor shook me, but there was something vaguely off about the look in her eyes. I felt like I had seen it before but couldn't place it.

Mary's face suddenly contorted and her lips snarled, "You're going to die."

I stared at her, my ears buzzing. I'd heard death threats

before, but her face was calm—calm enough to tell me she wasn't kidding. And her eyes glinted again in a way that sent fear straight to my heart.

I was going to die.

And then, I felt a searing pain move across my body and I collapsed to the ground, shaking. The last thing I saw before everything went black was Mary's smiling face and the stun gun in her hand.

TWENTY-TWO

I felt the hand on my head before I opened my eyes. It brushed my hair back softly and a warm cloth dabbed at my temple, which I suddenly realized was throbbing.

Where am I?

What happened?

And then it all came back to me.

"Mary!" I shrieked, opening my eyes and struggling to sit up.

"Shhhh," Slade said as he gently pushed me back down.

"Where are we? What's happening?" I said. My throat felt thick and stuffed with cotton and my midsection ached where Mary had tazed me.

"I—I don't know exactly where we are. But we're prisoners of the Octavians," Slade said. I noticed he had a long, jagged cut running down his cheek.

"But how?" None of this made any sense. I sat up, despite Slade's protests, and saw that we were alone in an ornately decorated room with a marble floor and gold and onyx carvings decorating the walls. Huge hieroglyphs crawled up the walls, dotted with shimmering jewels that stared menacingly down at us. At one end of the room was a wall of mirrors; at the other end, a huge half-human/half jackal statue, at least thirty feet tall, made of shiny black granite. It looked a lot like the dog-priest in the Book of the Dead; I shuddered as I realized that this was a god. He stared down at us with his crystal eyes, contemplating our fate.

Taking my eyes off the statue, I also noticed that the room was completely closed off, with no discernible door or window to escape through.

No problem. Slade can just shift us out of here.

"I can't," he said, reading my thoughts. He held up his wrists and I saw there were metal handcuffs on them. Metal weakened the Créatúir. They couldn't shift or use any power when directly touching it. "Someone or something grabbed me as I tried to shift back to my world after I saw you last night. I've been here since then."

"How did they know? Who did this?" I whispered.

Before Slade could answer, a portion of the floor rose up and Mary stepped out of the makeshift elevator, flanked by two Octavians. She stepped in front of us and we struggled to stand up.

She smiled, and her teeth were suddenly small and pointy like a ferret's. Her eyes glinted again—that same look I'd seen in the hallway—and, too late, I realized what she was.

She was Asher.

"What the—?" I screamed as I tried to lunge at him, but Slade held me back, even with his hands handcuffed.

Mary threw her head back and laughed. Her outside body peeled away and Asher stepped out of the skin, like he'd unzipped it, and it vanished.

"What have you done?" Slade asked quietly. His voice was measured, but for the first time ever, I heard fear.

Asher crossed his arms over his chest and smiled, a creepy, deep, mushy expression that made his features contort. "You never deserved to be king, Slade. You're a..." He pointed a long finger at me; it moved toward me, sharp as a knife, before retracting. "You're a traitor to your kind."

Slade shook his head but didn't say anything. I suddenly suspected that it wasn't the first time he'd heard that statement. I'd never stopped to think about what our relationship might look like to the Créatúir...or what Slade might have to put up with from his own kind in order to be with me. I suppose I always thought his parents were the only ones who objected to our relationship.

Asher took a step toward me, the creepy smile still on his face. "Although, I have to hand it to you—you certainly chose a human with, say, extraordinary gifts. Too bad for you that someone like me realized her value." He leered, looking me up and down. Slade stepped protectively in front of me.

But Asher reached around Slade, who couldn't brush him aside due to the metal handcuffs, and grabbed my upper arm, hard. "C'mon. My clients have been waiting a long time for this."

"Ow!" I shrieked as his long claws dug into my skin.

"Get away from her!" Slade tried to hit Asher with his bound arms, but was stopped, like he was moving through concrete. Then Asher flicked his finger, and Slade went sliding across the floor and slammed into one of the gold and pearl columns in the center of the room. Asher flicked his finger upward, and Slade rose into the air, slamming back onto the marble floor with a sickening crunch. He moaned and lay still, eyes closed.

"Stop! I'll come with you—just stop." Big fat tears started to fall down my face. I brushed at them and saw my hand was black.

I glanced at the gilded mirror on the back wall and sucked in my breath. Thick black eyeliner ringed my eyes and swirled up around my temples. My hair was braided, and woven with pearls and gold flecks.

They'd done me up to look just like her.

"Let's go, queen," Asher said. He shoved me toward the floor elevator.

I felt the sensation of going down. The door opened into a long, dark hallway. It was illuminated by a few torches, which cast shadows that seemed to be alive on the rock walls. Asher shoved me into a room that had only a long bench in it. A white robe and headdress hung on the wall.

"Put that on and someone will come for you." He pressed a button and the door sealed behind him.

With shaking hands, I put the robe and headdress on. I slipped my feet into gold sandals with pearls. I figured if I just did whatever they wanted for now—and if I could stall them at all—there might be enough time for Declan and the Order to find me and get us out of here. We had to be in the Alexandrian museum, and I could only hope that the team going after the Book really would come sooner rather than later.

Asher reappeared, threw me into another elevator, and then we were in a huge room with a domed ceiling. Around the perimeter of the room were pairs of gold sphinxes joined by the tail. In the center of the room was a large pool of perfectly still, shallow water that shone like glass. A pedestal with a platform rose from the center of the water. A group of five people, three men and two women, surrounded the pedestal—on which lay a scroll. Open.

Cleopatra's Book of the Dead.

My heart began to race and my knees went weak as Asher led me toward them. They considered me, as if looking at lobster in a fish tank and trying to decide if it was were big enough to eat. Asher yanked me down a pathway through the pool of water, toward the platform.

"Finally," one of the women said. She, like the others, was dressed in white robes and headdresses. We looked like we could all be transported back to ancient Egypt and completely blend in.

My eyes fixed on the guy to her right as my brain tried to figure out what the hell was going on. His deep blue eyes stared at me.

"Declan?" I said in a cracked voice.

How could he?

What was going on?

Is he ... behind all of this?

He smiled and shook his head. "I'm Grant, Declan's twin brother. So how is my wimpy, traitorous brother?"

"What?" Declan hadn't mentioned that his brother was also his twin, but I guessed that didn't mean it couldn't be true. I squinted at the man and realized that while at first glance he looked like Declan, his eyes were set a little closer together and his jaw was wider.

"Declan and I were raised by the Octavians, until he decided he didn't want to have anything to do with achieving our goal—the goal that we have been destined to achieve—and jumped ship to the opposing team." Grant shook his head, his eyes dark, the exact same way I'd seen Declan do it.

"Not the opposing team, the *true* team," I shouted. "The team your parents were on."

Grant gave me a hard look and then smiled in a way that chilled my bones. He looked to his left, to a man with short, graying hair and a deep tan who looked slightly familiar. "I think you raised us pretty well, Uncle Paul."

Paul shook his head and leered at me. "All this trouble just for you, young lady."

I swallowed hard. It was the archaeologist from the news. So that was why Declan never wanted to talk about his family. "Well, history isn't going to repeat itself," I said.

Grant smirked. "Octavian won the war—Cleopatra was defeated. Mark Antony, too. They had their shot at world domination and they failed. Because of Octavian, the Roman Empire grew in strength and contributed more to the world than you can possibly imagine. We are just continuing that legacy." The other Octavians nodded in agreement.

"Legacy? I don't think so." I shook my head.

"You're one to talk about legacy," Paul said, his voice stony. He glanced at Grant. "Surely you've heard that Mark Antony was to be reincarnated at the same time as Cleopatra?" He smiled, his teeth perfectly white and straight. "Two lost lovers, reunited."

Grant laughed and grabbed his lapels, chest puffed out. "Nice to see you again," he said to me.

I tried to make a neutral sound but it came out like a strangled scream. *No way.* I started to shake my head when Grant spoke.

"It's true. What, my brother didn't tell you? Or did you

think he was your lost love?" He chuckled and I felt a wave of nausea begin to build.

Grant is Mark Antony reincarnated, I told myself in disbelief. *And instead of protecting me, like he did in the last life, he chose to betray me in this one.*

There was a pause, and the air crackled around us.

"Surprise," Grant added softly. He extended a hand toward me. "My queen." He took a long, mocking bow. "Last chance to join the right side." He gestured to the open space next to him. "Cleopatra was supposed to work for Octavian, you know. She was his prisoner of war, but took the easy way out. It's your choice again: work with us or against us."

They all stared at me silently, and I suddenly felt like that lobster again. A long tear of sweat moved down my back and my hair started to plaster to the back of my neck under the heavy headdress.

"More than two thousand years later, my answer is the same: screw off," I said.

Grant rolled his eyes and sighed. One of the women gestured toward the Book, and Asher poked me from behind with something sharp. "Read that first section," the woman ordered.

I walked toward the Book, trying to figure out how to stall. As I looked down at it, a rushing feeling surged from my toes to my head, as if something was flooding me with power and magic. My head felt light and my fingertips buzzed and sparked.

"Don't you think I should wait?" I asked. "I don't have control over my powers at all yet. Shouldn't I wait and train more, so I don't do something crazy like raise a bunch of dead squirrels?"

The woman's face crumpled and she shook her head. "We don't have time for that. We wanted to wait, but the Order proved stronger than we'd calculated, so we must do it now."

"And if I refuse?" I couldn't help but ask.

"Then they're as good as dead. We will kill them one by one until you agree." She smiled, and I knew she was talking about my sisters. My family. Slade.

I gazed at the Book, my shoulders shaking. The hieroglyphs glinted with gold as if begging me to read them. I began to feel lightheaded, like I was somehow being hypnotized. While the Order had focused on my stress reactions, and worried that the Octavians might force me to read from the Book by threats or torture, no one had ever mentioned the possibility of being coerced into reading the Book *by the Book itself.*

I swallowed hard and prayed for protection. Still trying to resist, I cleared my throat and pretended to be concentrating on the translations. I kept thinking that if I waited a little longer, maybe someone or something would save us.

But the only sound was my heart pounding in my chest.

Then I heard myself start to speak. I kept my voice soft

at first, hoping that if I didn't say the words too loudly, they wouldn't work.

The air around me began to whirl, lifting the hair off my head and pulling at my robes. I read to the last line and closed my eyes, my knees shaking.

And then I heard them.

Moaning softly, making scratching noises like scampering mice. I opened my eyes and saw ghouls and corpses erupting from the floor—the undead. Their white blue eyes stared hungrily at me; their tattered clothes trailed on the ground. They headed straight for us, arms outstretched.

"Stop them!" Grant yelled.

"I can't!" I shrieked.

"Transfer your control to us!" the woman screamed as one of the undead pulled at her hair, opening its mouth to reveal rotting, bloody stumps for teeth.

"I don't know how!" I screamed. "I told you that!"

Grant ran forward and pointed to another spot, farther down on the scroll. "I think this spell will do it. Read!"

"No!" I said. It was my last bargaining chip. The undead didn't seem interested in me, only in everyone else, probably since I was the one who had raised them.

"No?" Grant gestured at Asher, who pressed a button. Slade appeared from the floor in one of those elevators. He was barely conscious, lying on the ground with long cuts all down his face. "He dies first," Grant said.

I screamed the words from the Book and put my palms

toward Grant, to transfer my power to him, as the undead lumbered closer to us. I closed my eyes and waited to be killed, maimed, eaten.

But the room suddenly went silent. I slowly opened my eyes and saw the undead all lined up, in soldier fashion, facing Grant and waiting for their first command.

"Bravo!" Paul clapped his huge hands together.

"Payment," Asher said, and held his hand out.

The other woman nodded and tossed Asher a vial.

"Thirsty for some hemlock?" Asher asked as he tipped Slade's head back and squeezed a few drops into his mouth. Slade's face turned black and his body went limp on the floor.

Poison.

"No!" I tried to run to Slade, but Grant pushed me to my knees and I collapsed forward, hitting my chin on the marble floor.

Asher walked over and patted my head. "There, there. Don't cry. After all, you're the one who did this to him. At least, that's what everyone in the Other Realm is going to hear. That you could've saved him but didn't."

I looked up at Asher, tears streaming down my face, but couldn't say anything. I watched as Slade gasped for breath, our eyes focused on each other.

The undead silently faced the Octavians, breathing heavily as they waited for a command. Out of the corner of my eye, I saw Grant walking toward me, dagger out.

I was no longer needed.

I kept my gaze focused on Slade and waited. His dark, glittering eyes focused intensely, and then a light quickly flashed over them. With a sudden move of his hands, he somehow found the strength to break the handcuffs on his wrists.

"Slade!" I screamed as I started to scramble toward him, away from Grant's dagger. "Get us out of here!" I knew he was weak, and that his powers couldn't last more than a few seconds.

But before I reached him, a brilliant white light blinded me. I landed with a crack, gashing my temple—on the sculpture of a sphinx. I was outside the Alexandrian museum.

Alone. Slade had shifted me out of danger, but he hadn't had enough power to shift himself.

He sacrificed himself for me.

I whispered his name, before the blood from my head ran down my face and everything went black.

TWENTY-THREE

The first thing I smelled was smoke. It burned the back of my throat and filled my lungs.

Am I dead?

I must be.

Or at least almost, mostly dead.

Will I ever see my sisters again?

My skin felt hot to the touch, but I didn't open my eyes. I knew everything was my fault, and I would just rather lie there until I died. To be put out of my misery.

I felt something cold dab at my forehead and I slowly opened my eyes. I saw Declan's clear blue eyes inches from my face, dirt streaks across his cheeks.

I struggled to sit up, but he shook his head and pressed

a cold cloth into my hand. I stared up at him, silently asking what happened.

He closed his eyes slowly and looked away. I glanced around. We were on the floor of what looked like the library at the compound, but there was sparking debris everywhere and charred furniture. The sky above us was thick with smoke and ashes fell down on us like it was raining fire.

"Where is everyone?" I whispered. "What happened?"

Declan looked back at me and I saw the tears in his eyes. "We woke up to the fire alarm, and immediately saw that you were missing. At first, we thought maybe you were with Slade."

The mention of Slade's name was like a knife to my stomach. Panic began to bubble up through my body, but I pressed my lips into a thin line as I let him finish.

"We didn't find any note, so we knew you'd been kidnapped. And we had to get moving—the Octavians had set the whole compound on fire." He gestured around him at the debris and ashes. "I left them all here to fight the fires and flagged a taxi to the museum—where I found you outside, unconscious. I brought you back here, thinking the fire would be out and we could keep you safe, but..." His voice cracked and he shook his head.

I didn't want to ask, but I had to. "What happened to... I mean, where is..."

Declan shook his head and put a hand over his eyes.

They were gone. Burned in the fire. All of them.

The compound was in ruins. Everyone in the Order was dead.

Declan cleared his throat. "But you got away from them. How did you manage that?"

My lips cracked as I whispered, "I didn't. Slade shifted me out."

"What happened to him?"

I put my face in my hands and shook my head. "I—I'm not sure. He's hurt. Badly." I couldn't bring myself to say my worst fear out loud: that he worse than hurt.

"Oh. I'm sorry."

I couldn't look at him. "There's more. I escaped, but not before they got what they wanted. Declan, I read from the Book. They have their army now."

He stood up and stumbled backward, almost falling into a still-smoking pile of wood that looked like conference room chairs. "How *could* you?"

"I didn't have a choice!" I screamed, throwing my hands in the air. "The Book made me! And then they were going to kill Slade and everyone else if I didn't turn control of the army over to them!"

"They may have killed him in any case," he said.

I jumped up. "I have to find out what happened to Slade before I do anything else." I looked frantically around. "Phone?"

Declan gave me a long, disapproving look before tossing me his cell phone. Leah answered on the second ring.

"Have you heard about Slade?" I asked quickly.

"Rhea? Where are you? Are you still in Egypt?" Her voice crackled over the long-distance connection. "Wait—what happened to Slade?"

"It's … it's a long story. Just know that Asher betrayed him and gave him poison. He tried … " My voice broke. "He saved me but he couldn't save himself."

"What's going on? Are you safe?" Leah was measuring her words carefully.

"Please, just find out what happened to Slade. Tell me he's going to be okay," I whispered.

There was a long pause, and I could practically hear her debating whether she should interrogate me or send over some kind of spy to report back to her. But thankfully she agreed. "I'll head to Inis Mor right now and find out what I can."

I tossed the phone back to Declan and took a deep breath. "We have to get out of here. It's not safe."

He nodded, and when he turned to leave I saw that his back was streaked with blood. "That looks pretty awful." I gingerly lifted his shirt and saw burn marks on his lower back. "We need to have that bandaged up."

After some initial protest, he agreed and we called a taxi. On the way to the hospital, we made up a story about how trying to light a cigar had gone terribly wrong. In the emergency room, we waited behind a small curtain for the doctors to clean and bandage Declan's burns. Every sound made our muscles tense, since we expected the Octavians to come crashing through and swoop us up.

When, after two hours, we were still safe, I exhaled. "What are we going to do?" I asked quietly, ripping apart a cotton ball.

Declan tried to shift on the edge of the hospital bed, but he winced in pain. "We're screwed."

"No, I—"

He cut me off with a withering look. "They have the army. They're unstoppable. The Order's headquarters are gone. Your boyfriend might be dead."

"He's not dead!" I shrieked. A nurse poked her head in and I gave her an apologetic smile. "He's not dead. I can feel it, okay?" I hissed. I swallowed down the fear that told me there was no way he could have survived a direct ingestion of hemlock.

"Sorry," Declan said. He leaned forward and gingerly put his hands on the bed, studying the blue and white tile floor. "I just don't know what to do. If there's anything we *can* do."

"We'll figure something out," I said, just as the doctor finally reappeared with gauze and tape. I looked away as they began cleaning Declan's burns. I heard him suck in his breath at the pain several times.

"I assume my brother told you?" he said in a strangled voice. I looked up and saw that they were applying some kind of salve to his back.

"About him being Mark An—Mark?" I quickly stopped

myself. The last thing I needed was the doctor overhearing and committing me to the psych ward.

He slowly nodded his head. "The first-born son." He smiled ruefully. "Grant was born one minute before me."

One minute.

I nodded, but I couldn't get the thought out of my head that fate had intervened by just one minute. If Declan had been born first, none of this would have happened.

If the fire alarm had gone off one minute earlier, the Order might have been able to put out the fire in the compound.

If Slade had broken out of his handcuffs one minute earlier, we both might have escaped.

It certainly seemed like the course of history was dictated not by huge battles or important decrees, but by small, intimate moments, rippling one minute at a time.

TWENTY-FOUR

It was nighttime by the time we left the hospital. The streets were beginning to fill, with couples strolling the sidewalks and groups of tourists heading to dinner. There seemed to be a sea of people everywhere, and all the signs were written in Arabic. Although I was able to read ancient Egyptian, thanks to some broken piece of DNA that remained, that language had largely disappeared from the world—now everything was in Arabic, which I didn't know at all.

We walked to a nearby hotel, paying for it with the last of Declan's money. We only had enough for one room, and even though it felt really awkward to be in a hotel room with Declan by myself, there was no other choice. I perched uncomfortably on the bed while he took a seat at the small table next to the window that overlooked a crowded Alexandrian street filled with bicycles, food vendors, and robed figures.

"So what are we going to do?" I asked impatiently. I picked at a hangnail, my thoughts still with Slade. I wished I could just enter Inis Mor like my sister and find out what was happening with him.

"I don't know." Declan closed his eyes and tried to lean back, grimacing.

"What about if we snuck into the Octavians' headquarters and got the Book back? Maybe there's a spell in there to get rid of the undead."

"And what if there's not?" he snapped, his eyes still closed. "Besides, there's only two of us. We could never get inside."

"Well, Cleopatra snuck into Julius Caesar's palace while rolled up in a rug, didn't she?" I shouted. She'd been unrolled in Caesar's throne room and asked to be restored to power in Egypt. It saved her life and her country. I'd read about it during my study session with Mary ... for all the good that did me.

"Get a grip on yourself. You're sounding crazy," Declan said evenly. "That's a terrible plan."

I opened my mouth to protest, but I knew he was right. "Okay, so what else?" I asked quietly.

He shook his head and put his hands in his pockets. "Nothing else. Square one."

I shook my head furiously. "No way. We have to do

something—now. We don't have time to wait. Since we obviously can't figure out how to kill the undead, we need to do something else. We need to raise some soldiers ourselves, to fight against theirs." As much as I didn't like the idea of commanding an army of brain-eaters, I couldn't think of any other way to stop the Octavians.

Declan gave me a long look. "You need some sleep." He started to turn away, but I reached out and grabbed his arm. "How in the world would we do that without the Book?" he asked.

"I don't know, but we can figure it out. There's nothing else we can do. We have to fight back!"

Declan turned to me and shook his head. "Not happening."

I clenched my fists and set my jaw. *He doesn't know what he's doing. He's scared, just like I am.*

But I didn't say any of that. I said something that I knew would hurt him.

"Maybe you are just like your brother," I spat out. I stood up and stomped over to the bathroom, slamming the door shut. I stayed there for an hour, expecting him to knock on the door and try to work out a plan. But he never did. So I slowly opened the door a crack and saw that he was asleep on the floor next to the bed. I crept over to the window to close the shades, but the enormous full moon caught my eye.

It seemed hard to imagine that it was the same moon that had stood watch over Cleopatra.

I'm not giving up. There has to be a way.
With or without Declan.

———

I lay in bed that night, tossing and turning, unable to sleep. Declan snored on the floor next to the bed as I listened to the sounds of Alexandria outside. The car horns and distant shouting made me feel like I'd never been further from Cleopatra.

I had nothing. I didn't know what had happened to Slade. The Octavians had their army. The Order's headquarters, and all the knowledge it contained, had burned to the ground. My family was thousands of miles away. Declan didn't want to help me.

And all of it seemed to be my fault.

I kept my eyes open and stared at the ceiling, hoping sleep would just suddenly happen. I couldn't close my eyes—each time I did, I saw the panting, rotting Octavian army marching across the sand.

I have to find a way to fight back. Help me. Help me find a way.

———

The dream started immediately. It was the same as before— I was Cleopatra, playing Senet in the bedchamber. Except it was on fast-forward, and my movements were quick, my speech unintelligible. Iras rushed over to the door and let the High Priestess inside. Then everything slowed down and moved like molasses on a hot Egyptian day.

"The carvings are in place," the High Priestess said laboriously, in a deep voice.

"What do they say? Where are they?" My tongue felt thick and the words large and cumbersome.

The High Priestess slowly glanced at Iras. "All of the powers of Isis, Your Highness. The gods will keep them safe in the most holy of places until your return."

I woke up with a gasp. My hair was plastered to the side of my face in long, sweaty streaks.

All the powers of Isis. What does that mean?

I leaned down and shook Declan's shoulder, hard. He woke and gave me a dirty look.

"What?"

"What does 'all the powers of Isis' mean?" I whispered.

He shook his head and rubbed his eyes as he sat up. "I have no idea what you're talking about."

"I had a dream," I said impatiently, twisting the bed sheet around in my hands. "The High Priestess came to me and told me there are carvings, which hold all the power of Isis, in place for my return—which I'm assuming means reincarnation."

Declan gave me a long look, eyes narrowed. "It could mean anything, but maybe it means you could access the power of Isis through carvings of spells or incantations."

He slowly stood up and crossed his arms. "Are you sure that's what she said?"

I nodded emphatically. "So the spells from the Book might be carved somewhere else?"

"It's certainly possible that Cleopatra had a safety net, another place to access her powers should something happen to the Book." Declan raised his hands, palms up. "But I can't imagine where they would be. There's no way they could have survived the past two thousand years."

I sighed. "'The most holy of places,'" I muttered. "Wait —" My heart started racing. "Could the most holy of places mean a temple? Like a church?"

Declan leaned against the desk in front of the window. "Of course."

"Didn't I read somewhere that pieces of the Temple of Isis were found recently?" I quickly tucked my hair behind my ears and sat up straighter on the bed.

Declan raised his eyebrows. "Well, yes. Pylons—a kind of support beam located in the center of the structure— were recovered from the water."

"Do we know if there are any carvings or symbols on them?"

"I'm not sure. I think so," he said.

I clapped my hands together. "It's worth a shot, right? What if the spell to raise the dead is also carved on the remains from the temple?"

He frowned, his features dark. "There are two problems

with your theory. One, you assume that raising an army of the undead to battle the Octavians is a good plan. Two, even if I agreed with you—which I don't, for the record—it's impossible to access the pylons."

Ignoring his first statement, I said, "Why?"

"Because the pylons are held at the Alexandrian museum, just above the Octavians' headquarters."

I collapsed forward onto the bed and buried my face in the sheet. Of course they were. But I knew I couldn't give up. I sat up and squarely looked at him. "So let's disguise ourselves and head there tomorrow." When he opened his mouth to protest, I held up my hand. "Unless you have a better idea."

He sat back down on the floor and said, "Fine. But let's give it one more day for everything to settle down. Now that they've finished with you, you're nothing but a threat to them. They'd still like to see you—both of us—deader than their soldiers once were."

I had waited for over two thousand years to defeat the Octavians. I supposed I could wait one more day.

TWENTY-FIVE

"Would you sit down? You're going to give me a coronary." Declan stared out the window, drumming his fingers against the table in our hotel room.

I threw myself down on the bed in an exaggerated flounce, but he didn't seem to care. It was only mid-afternoon, but it was already the longest day of my life. We couldn't leave the room for fear of an Octavian spotting us, so we barricaded ourselves inside and stared at each other. We couldn't even watch television since nothing was in English.

I spent the morning watching a man outside with a long black beard yelling at his car, whose engine was smoking. Then a bird flew by two or three times. Next, Declan stared at his hands for an hour. At that point, I tried to take a nap but my adrenaline was pumping too much.

I wanted desperately to be able to call Leah and ask if she had heard about Slade, but I was suddenly worried that the Octavians would track us that way. So I paced and prayed for a messenger from the Other Realm to appear and tell me what was happening. Finally, I started to go crazy and opted for small talk.

"What's your girlfriend like?" I asked Declan.

His eyes flicked to me and he hesitated before exhaling loudly. His shoulders went limp. "Hannah's great. She's an education major and wants to be a first grade teacher someday. She knows nothing about all of this. She's so ... normal." He looked at me critically, gauging my reaction.

I nodded in understanding. "I get it. Believe me, normal sounds awesome right now."

He pulled his phone out and tapped at it before handing it to me. "That's her."

"Whoa." She was a tiny, tanned blonde with perfect skin and flawless makeup. "She's really pretty," I said, handing the phone back to him.

"Thanks." A small, genuine smile appeared on his face. It was so odd to think of him doing regular things like going to the movies and cooking dinner rather than scowling or drilling me on hieroglyphic translations.

There was a long pause as I searched for another discussion topic. Something. Anything other than the deafening silence that tugged at my sanity.

"If you could have any food right now, what would it

be?" I said. I closed my eyes and thought of frosty, ice cold glasses of lemonade. A slushie. A Gatorade so cold it had chunks of ice still in it.

Declan smiled and glanced out the window. "A cheeseburger. The kind where the cheese is melted to the bun and the whole thing almost falls apart in your hands every time you take a bite."

"Not my first choice, but understandable." I sighed and pulled my sweaty curls off my neck.

"At school, there's a restaurant in town called the Big Cheese and all they serve is cheeseburgers. Those burgers single-handedly got me through finals last year."

I tried to picture him and Hannah eating cheeseburgers and studying. "What are you majoring in?"

He gave a low chuckle. "Accounting."

"Seriously?" I thought all accountants were little old men who sat in rooms and crunched numbers.

"Yep. Math has always come easily to me, and its simplicity and decisiveness are weirdly comforting. There's very little room to wrongly interpret an equation." He cleared his throat. "It's black and white, and everything makes sense."

I nodded. "Like with the Egyptians."

He looked at me in surprise.

"See? I did pay attention to you. Sometimes." He laughed and I looked down at my hands. "Can I ask you something?"

"Sure." His voice caught in his throat.

"How did you find out about your parents? That they

were really in the Order, not with the Octavians? Didn't they have the tattoo?" I looked at Declan's neck tattoo, the black eye with a lightning-bolt tear. I couldn't picture a little kid having any idea about secret societies.

He shook his head. "They didn't have the tattoo due to the nature of my mom's work. As far as me finding out about them—I don't know if you remember this, but Mark Antony and Cleopatra's children were raised by the Octavians. So while the Order existed to protect Mark Antony's legacy, but his blood relatives—his children—were raised in the enemy sect."

I nodded again. I did remember reading that, but never thought about the implications. I shivered at the thought of their children being brought up by the Octavians—by the very people who'd killed them.

"Well, one of their children, Selene, secretly joined the Order when she grew up. She passed on a lot of the Octavians' secret scrolls. One revealed that all members of the Octavians were to have a special gold coin with a cobra on it, a calling card of sorts, to identify themselves. My parents died when I was five, but I do have a distinct memory of my father showing me a picture of the gold coin and saying that if someone presented one to me—if they asked me to accept that coin—I was to know that their true intentions were evil."

"So what happened?" I prompted.

"My uncle raised us to be Octavians, but never mentioned the coins. Until I turned sixteen, when he presented me with one of them. My blood just ran cold. I knew then that everything he'd told me was a lie, and so I sought out the Order—which he'd told me was my sworn enemy. John and the others filled in the gaps, confirming that my parents were really aligned with them." His voice wavered at the mention of the Order.

"I'm so sorry," I whispered. My throat began to burn as I thought of everyone who was gone. "Did you ever think of just leaving all this behind? I mean, you could've just stayed at school and lived a regular life. Didn't you ever think about just ignoring the appearance of the Star of Duat?"

He softly chuckled. "I'm sure I did, at one point. But history has always fascinated me—the idea that where we come from shapes who we are today, and the idea that if just one thing long ago was different, the entire world would look different. People might not have been born, cities would be unformed, discoveries unmade." He paused. "I guess I inherited that from my mom. I wasn't okay with just sitting on the sidelines."

"Do you think your brother will ever come around?"

"I hope so, someday. When all of this is over, I hope we can find common ground. We're twins, so there's a lot to choose from." Declan's voice cracked and I wanted to rush over and hug him. But I knew it would just make him more uncomfortable, so I stayed on the bed and counted the hours.

———

Finally, night fell and we were one step closer to entering the museum. Declan decided to take a shower, and I sat alone on the bed, thinking of Slade. I heard a rustle in the corner of the room and the tiny hairs on the back of my neck pricked up. Someone else was in the room with me.

I whirled around, expecting to see a member of the Octavians hurtling my way, but it was Caiside, Slade's mother.

"What are you doing here?" I whispered. I quickly stood up and smoothed down my wrinkled white T-shirt and blue shorts. I glanced around nervously, remembering that the last time we met, she all but hand-delivered me to the Octavians.

"Don't fear. I am here with news about my son," she said slowly, surveying me up and down like a piece of meat gone rancid.

I pressed my hands to my stomach. "What happened?" My voice caught in my throat as it tightened.

The seconds before she answered were the longest of my life. "He is very sick, but still with us."

I let out an exhale and fell against the bed, breathing heavily. "He's alive?"

"Yes." Her face was hard, and I suddenly realized that she hadn't come here of her own volition.

"Can I see him?" My hands shook and I felt lightheaded.

Her mouth pressed into a firm line. "No. He is recovering

at the palace in Inis Mor and it is best that he be allowed to rest. His survival is still not definite."

I thought of him alone, lying on a bed, potentially wasting away, and I cursed the beige hotel room where I was stuck playing out a role destined for me long before I was born.

"He woke briefly and told us what happened. He also asked that someone visit your world and tell you that he's alive. He wants to send Créatúir guards to protect you." She narrowed her eyes at me and frowned.

I shook my head. "No. I can't have anyone else—human or Créatúir—getting hurt on my account." I shuddered as I thought of the burning embers of the Order's headquarters. "Too many lives have already been lost."

Caiside studied me for a moment and I thought I saw the faintest glint of an approving look in her dark eyes. "Very well. I will relay the message."

She turned to shift back to her realm, and I stood up and rushed forward. Without thinking, I reached forward and grabbed her hands. She shrunk back in horror and looked at me with disgust. "Please," I said. "Just tell him that I'm going to end all of this soon and we can be together."

She shook her head. "Mixing of the races has never ended well." She paused. "But I will tell him. He is the king, after all." With that, she disappeared.

The wisps of Other Realm sparkle were barely gone when Declan emerged from the bathroom, his hair wet. I was beyond thankful that he didn't appear while Caiside was there—I could only imagine what she'd tell Slade.

"Were you talking to yourself?" he asked.

"Yes," I said quickly. I elbowed around him and headed to the bathroom. "My turn to shower." Once inside the bathroom, I exhaled slowly and the tears started to roll down my cheeks.

Slade is alive. He made it. He fought through being poisoned. Now, it's my turn to fight.

TWENTY-SIX

The next day, I sucked my breath in hard as we stepped into the lobby of the hotel. What felt like millions of people crushed in around me. Back when I'd first arrived in Egypt, I'd been guarded, isolated, and escorted by the Order in a relatively comfortable way. Now Declan and I were among the masses, and I got shoved and poked with elbows about sixty times as we made our way through the insanity of the hotel lobby.

I wore a burka, like I had before. It wasn't necessary that I wear it, but once again it was a perfect disguise. The second I'd put it on, in my room, I started burning up. The lobby of the hotel wasn't air conditioned—or at least it didn't seem like it—and my body temperature was rising to near boiling. My peripheral vision was down to almost nothing, and I felt like a sweaty blind girl being lead to her execution.

"We're almost outside," Declan whispered as he held on to my elbow. With his dark hair, he blended in with the crowd, and my black outfit ensured that I did too. We probably just looked like two people traveling through Egypt—and not two Americans ready to save the world with a little help from a fantastical force.

We got outside, but the fresh air did little to relax me. It was stifling, almost unbearable, and it took everything for me not to rip off my outfit and gulp down a bottle of water.

"The Alexandrian museum," Declan said as we settled into a cab outside the hotel.

It still seemed strange, to me, that the Octavians' headquarters were located underneath the museum. But I guess it made sense. They funded their operations by selling off antiquities, just as the Order did, and what better place to have their central location than right below where those artifacts were showcased. Still, it seemed weird that a place where history was supposed to be preserved and revered was sitting on top of a space that seemed devoted to destroying it.

I pressed my knees together and tightened my fists under the folds of the black robe as the taxi drove us through the crowded streets.

Courage. Be brave.

Draw strength from her.

The cab driver stopped in front of the sprawling museum,

made of intricate gray stonework and huge pillars. Declan paid in Egyptian pounds, and I swallowed quickly to keep from puking under the burka. I was already sweaty and uncomfortable. The last thing I needed to deal with was puke, too.

"I'll wait across the street while you go inside." Declan gestured toward the stairs, and I grunted. It was too risky for him to try to enter the museum. I scanned the crowd for a group that I could seamlessly join without suspicion. It would look strange to have me wandering around the museum by myself.

"There." Declan nodded toward a group of tourists, some wearing robes, walking up to the entrance together. I quickly stepped behind them and followed their lead. I tried to turn back and give Declan one final glance, but I was shoved from behind by the crowd.

It all starts here.

My heart was pounding as we entered the museum. I knew that I was entering the lion's den—that I was literally just steps away from people who wouldn't hesitate to kill me or worse. And I was choosing to do this.

Once inside, I followed the group through the ancient underwater excavations exhibit, my eyes quickly scanning the walls to see any hidden entrances or exits or anything out of place. But I didn't see anything unusual. Then, a flash went by my veil and my heart leapt into my throat.

It was an Octavian, standing against the wall, talking to a museum guard. I recognized him from the marketplace.

I wonder if they've spotted Declan outside.

I glanced down at my robe.

I wonder if they've spotted me.

The museum security guard started to slowly walk toward me, his eyes fixed on the mesh of my veil. I stood in place, frozen behind the tourists who were studying the museum map. I felt like I should take a fighting stance, or rip off my robe to fight more easily, but I was stuck.

Then, just as he reached me, he brushed past to the crowd behind me. He roughly grabbed a man who had his hands in his pockets and started shouting at him in Arabic. The man held up his hands, clearly not understanding. The security guard reached into the guy's pocket and pulled out a small Cleopatra statue. It was a souvenir from the gift shop.

"Shoplifter," I heard one of the tourists in front of me whisper as the man was roughly pushed toward the door.

I exhaled. My clothes were wet with sweat underneath my robes, and my hair was plastered to my head like a skullcap. But I kept going.

I walked through exhibit after exhibit, artifacts blurring together in a haze of gold, onyx, and lacquer. I decided to slowly make my way through each floor, like a regular tourist would, instead of heading straight for the pylons. Anything that might seem like I was overly interested in artifacts from Cleopatra's time could cause trouble, so I leisurely strolled each floor until all that was left was the antiquities wing.

My heart started to pound as I headed toward the mummies. I looked up and saw that I was standing underneath a banner with a picture of a mummy. There was a crowd gathered at the end of the hallway around a large structure. In the otherwise dim lighting, a spotlight shone upon a tall, sable-colored column.

I hitched up my robe and walked toward it. Long beads of sweat zigzagged down my back as the column grew taller and taller upon my approach.

"The pylon," I whispered, my neck craned upward. It stood over seven feet tall and must have weighed several tons. I remembered reading that it was carved out of red granite, but it was the color of a mink coat.

"It's so beautiful!" I exclaimed. A man next to me shot me a look of surprise and I realized I shouldn't speak at all; English would definitely give me away. Another man looked at me strangely, trying to peer into my veil, and I suddenly wished I had taken Slade's mother up on the offer to be surrounded by Créatúir guards.

I focused on scanning the pylon. I was hoping to quickly recognize the spell to raised the dead ... if it was even there. I stood very still, squinting at the large piece of granite that was more than two thousand years old, mouthing each symbol as I recognized it. I knew most of them, but there were a few that were unfamiliar.

After several minutes, I shook my head slightly, my stomach dropping. I didn't see the spell.

Maybe it wasn't on the pylon, or maybe I just didn't recognize it.

Tears sprang to my eyes as I tried to will it to appear. Nothing.

I turned toward the exit, ready to walk away into a likely disastrous future, but a glint from the top of the pylon caught my eye. It was like a tiny mirror reflecting sunlight. I wove through the crowd for a closer look. As I stood in front of the column, the reflection disappeared. No one else around me seemed to have seen it.

Through my veil, I could make out a line of hieroglyphs at the very top of the pylon. I instantly recognized it as the spell from the Book of the Dead.

It must have been carved at the top to be the closest to the gods.

My hands shaking and my head pounding, I silently memorized the lines of text. Then, I nodded and walked out of the museum, toward Declan.

We had the spell.

TWENTY-SEVEN

The desert was eerily still, the lights of Alexandria winking in the distance against the night sky. We'd paid a cab to drop us off far away from the city, no questions asked. It made sense to try out the spell far away from civilization, in case anything went wrong. If it worked, we'd contact the Octavians and tell them it was Go Time—they'd have to get through *our* army of the undead if they wanted to start building their empire.

I clutched the paper with the spell to my chest, trying to lower my blood pressure. I'd written it down the second I reached Declan outside the museum. Without even realizing it, I'd written it in hieroglyphs rather than English. Declan had murmured approvingly as he saw me sketching. Yet whether in English or ancient Egyptian, the spell was ours. All we had to do was find the courage to use it.

There were so many unknowns and what-ifs.

What if the spell didn't work, or the undead attacked us?

What if our army wasn't as strong as the Octavians' army?

What if one of us died?

What if we failed, and I let down not only the future, but the past as well?

But all those questions didn't matter. We had no other choice.

"Ready?" Declan asked.

I nodded and held the paper out in front of me. As I started to say the words, a gnawing feeling grew in my stomach. I wasn't sure if it was the power or just fear, but I kept going.

"*Alana …*" I faltered as the wind blew and a cloud of sand kicked up toward my face.

"Keep going," Declan urged, his eyes wide.

"*Alana, Abdu Heba, Libu, Ma'at, Menat, Tumilas, Unat!*" I declared.

The ground began to shake, and the sand started moving around, shifting and molting like it was alive. It spun around in a circle, forming a tornado that sparked and smoked before collapsing back onto the earth. A long, jagged crease appeared in the sand, like on pavement during an earthquake.

We waited, but nothing else happened.

"It didn't work," I said. I looked frantically at the paper. "Why didn't it work? It's the same spell. I remember it from…"

From when Slade almost died.

"Say it again!" Declan said. He put his hands on my shoulders. "Say it again," he said firmly.

I opened my mouth to start over when I heard it—a long, slow groan. My hand froze in the air, the spell clutched in my fingers. My eyes slowly slid to the crack in the earth. Declan's hands went limp on my shoulders and both of our bodies got immediate goose bumps.

A finger emerged, reaching up from the sand … a hand stretched toward the sky.

And then two. And then three.

One by one, they climbed out, glassy blue-white eyes staring at me, waiting for a command. Some were dressed in long white robes, some in regular clothes like blue jeans. A few wore suits and tuxedos, and a couple wore nothing at all. But they all breathed heavily, expelling clouds of grave dust into the air.

"Whoa," Declan said as he surveyed the undead, all in varying stages of decay. Yet they were definitely all under my command and waiting for my instructions. "Keep going. We need more."

"Er, stay!" I held my hand up like I was commanding a dog. Weird, but it worked. They stayed in place, glassy eyes trained on me.

We ran several feet over and repeated the spell. Again, there was a jagged crease in the earth and more undead popped up through it, lining up like soldiers.

Over and over we raised them, until we had enough to battle the Octavians' army. Declan and I stood on a small sand dune, surveying the lines of soldiers below us.

A strong, hot wind blew across the desert as I raised my hand. They bowed their heads in reverence.

Once again, I had command of an army. Once again, I had power.

"Rhea, look." Declan pointed to a figure in the distance.

I squinted and made out a stocky silhouette dressed in black. "Is that…?"

He nodded. "An Octavian. They must've spotted you at the museum and followed us here." He lifted his arm, fist clenched, in greeting. The Octavian turned and sprinted back toward a car, clearly to report back that we were ready for a fight.

"Now we wait," Declan said.

"We're ready," I said.

And this time, I wasn't giving up so easily.

———

The darkness of the desert surrounded us, the air filled with the sounds of the undead moaning and reaching out into the night. With our army in front of us, we waited. We could hear the Octavians marching toward us, and held out breaths as we strained to catch sight of them.

I clutched Declan's arm until my knuckles turned white. My knees were shaking. Even though this was my heritage—my destiny—nothing could have prepared me for this. At sixteen, I should've been thinking about buying a car, clothes, or failing a math test—not sending a self-raised army of the undead into battle to stop the end of the world.

"Let's do this," I said, my jaw set.

We were ready. Shoulder to shoulder, we turned toward the horizon. And then, they appeared. Marching toward us, moaning, limbs decaying, their crumbling fingers outstretched.

I sucked in my breath and fought the urge to scream or cry or run away. I wasn't going to give in the way she did. I was going to finally finish this.

Behind the Octavians' army was Grant, flanked by his Uncle Paul and the other Octavians. They wore black T-shirts and jeans, their arms folded across their chests.

The wind whipped between the two armies as the Octavians grew closer. I expected the Octavians' army to stop, to pause a moment before we battled, but they continued to approach.

"Declan?" I said nervously.

He stared off into the distance and shook his head. "We'll stand our ground. Let them come to us—let them tire out first."

I nodded, but the bile rose in my throat. We stood silently while they trudged toward us, ready to kill or be killed.

We will win.

There is no other choice.

Although I knew history wasn't in our favor. In Cleopatra and Antony's last battle, the Battle of Actium, they were overpowered by Octavian's army and had to retreat; they were later captured and committed suicide. Egypt fell, and Rome became an Empire.

History does not have to repeat itself.

The Octavians' army kept lumbering toward ours. We waited until they were an arm's length away, and then gave the command.

"Attack!" I shouted, and our army sprang into action below us. They stretched out their arms, ready to grab and claw and fight to the second death.

The armies met in a ball of hands, claws, teeth, and tearing flesh. They bit, scratched, and flailed at each other, killing by literally ripping one another to shreds. I swallowed hard as I felt vomit rise up in my throat at the grotesque scene.

Declan and I held our breaths, clutching each other's hands if only to stay standing. The armies seemed pretty evenly matched in numbers, but ours seemed more motivated ... they had more fire behind them.

Maybe it was because I'd raised them myself—the power of their commander wasn't diluted.

Or maybe it was something else.

"Look at their army. Why do their soldiers look so different from ours?" Declan said.

I studied the Octavians' army. Their undead *did* look different, even from two days ago. And they weren't as decayed or rotting as ours were. In fact, they looked like they'd been freshly killed. I swallowed hard as I realized how the Octavians had expanded their forces.

"They're actual people," I whispered in horror. "They're using modern people they've killed." After I raised the initial group, they must have allowed those undead to kill people, turning them into more undead to build their numbers. I felt lightheaded as I wondered if those deaths were my fault, too.

"How could you?" Declan screamed across the battlefield toward his brother and uncle. But we were too far away, and his words were carried away by the wind. Declan put his hands over his head and screamed wordlessly into the sky.

"Look!" I pointed. Our army was moving through the crowd, dispatching the Octavians' soldiers. They were fighting with passion and purpose, imbued with the power of Isis. Even though they were outnumbered, our army was dispatching two to their one, until the numbers were almost evenly matched.

We stood silently, our mouths open, as they continued to fight. After a few more minutes, a wind blew across the desert, and the only thing between the Octavians and ourselves was a sea of bodies on the ground.

The undead had killed each other.

The sand rustled around them, rising into the air like a wall. It folded neatly over the bodies and swallowed them whole. Another wind blew, and the sand smoothed out—and it was like nothing had happened.

And then all that was left were those of us who had inherited history.

☥
TWENTY-EIGHT

How did you raise your own army without the Book?" Grant screamed at us. He looked at Paul, who shook his head in disbelief.

"Wouldn't you like to know!" I shouted back, hands on my hips.

"It's over, Grant," Declan said. We stood shoulder to shoulder on the dune, our feet planted in the sand.

"So says you!" Grant clenched his fists and started to charge toward us, but quickly realized he was alone. He glanced back at Paul and the other Octavians. "What are you waiting for?" They looked at one another and took a few steps backward, then began hurrying back toward their vehicles. Grant slowly turned to us, a defeated look on his face.

But then he started running again, this time with more

determination. He dashed straight toward me, the Book of the Dead in one hand, a knife in the other.

Declan stepped in front of me. "Get back!" he shouted. He crouched down, waiting for his brother.

As Grant raced toward us, my entire body tensed. He threw himself on Declan, and the Book fell to the sand. Grant pressed his dagger to Declan's throat; yet even though they were twins, Declan was clearly the stronger. He flung his brother onto the sand and wrenched the dagger away from him. He held it to Grant's chest, hesitating.

"Destroy the Book!" he shouted to me.

I sprang to action, scooping up the Book and shaking it open. My fingers burned with magic as I ran my hand down it. The swirling hieroglyphs tempted me, but I focused on scanning the text, looking for the destruction spell that I knew must be there.

"I think this is it!" I screamed. In one spell, I'd immediately recognized the hieroglyphs for "destroy." I started muttering the words, and the Book began to smoke. My fingertips burned and I jumped back a little, glancing at Declan and Grant.

Grant was still on the ground, struggling against Declan's knife. But Declan couldn't kill his brother.

I was about to mutter the last word and end it all when Grant leaned forward and threw Declan off with all his might. I saw the glint of a second knife blade, and before I could move, Grant drove the knife into Declan's shoulder.

I screamed the last word of the spell, and the Book caught on fire. I dropped it and raced over to Grant, shoving him as hard as I could. The blade of his knife caught my arm, sending a long, jagged cut down it.

"Declan!" I struggled to pull him up, our blood mixing together on the sand. He met my gaze with his deep blue eyes, then turned toward his brother and crouched down in an attack stance.

Grant came at him again and wrapped his arms around his brother, tackling him to the ground. They wrestled, sand spitting everywhere, as the sickening sound of bone hitting bone echoed through the desert.

I was so focused on them that I didn't see Paul climbing up the sand dune behind us, knife in hand.

"All hail the queen," he said. I whirled around. He stood ten feet away from me, smiling. He waved a knife around in the air. "This is going to be too easy. Start running. It'll be more fun that way."

With no better options, I glanced toward the city, wondering if the sand would slow me down. But I didn't get a chance to run before Paul tackled me, knocking the wind out of me. Gasping for breath, I looked up. He was smiling, and holding the knife high in the air.

I closed my eyes and prayed my death would be quick. Then I heard her voice.

I failed once. Don't fail again.
Call on Isis.

My fingers began to burn, and I clutched a handful of desert sand—it seemed to be mixed with ashes from the Book. I squeezed it as tightly as I could, and it began to glimmer and spark; I felt it turning into tiny blades of glass. I threw it in Paul's face.

The shards cut into his eyes, making blood run down his cheeks. He dropped his knife and clutched his head. "I'm blind!"

I wrenched myself upward, glancing at Declan in time to see him throw Grant over his shoulder onto the sand, knocking him out with that final blow. Declan spotted me and started running.

"Come on!" he shouted, pointing to the lights of Alexandria. We ran full speed toward the city—for almost an hour—and never looked back. We ran on pure adrenaline; even Declan's injured shoulder didn't slow him down. I didn't know if any of the Octavians were following us, but as soon as I saw the pink granite sphinx that guards Alexandria, I knew we were safe.

I took refuge in the city that was once home to a great queen, which she gave her life to protect. Just as the Mediterranean whispered the secrets of her fallen kingdom, it watched as we'd battled again.

With the warm Alexandrian breeze lifting the hair off my neck, I found a phone. As soon as my mother answered, I said, "I can home come now."

I dreamt of her again on my way home from Egypt.

I was in the bedchamber that I'd seen in my other visions, but this time I was myself within the dream, standing there looking at her. She sat on her gold throne with its pearl and onyx carvings, regarding me with her kohl-rimmed eyes. On her head was a tall crown, and she wore brilliant robes of deep blue and red.

She lifted a hennaed hand and beckoned me forward. I took a step, cringing at how my flip-flops smacked against the marble floor. She held up her hand, palm facing me. I slowly brought my hand up and pressed it into hers. A warmth spread between our hands, an electric current humming softly. It ran down my arm and up through my head.

"You have done what I could not," she whispered in Greek, her native tongue.

"Yes. It is over," I replied in English.

She smiled, her bright red lips full of joy. "But your story is not over. Your loved one is royalty."

I shook my head. Slade may have been named king of Inis Mor, but I could never have been his queen—even *if* that had been a possible scenario. I'd seen what power could do, and what it could destroy. I didn't know what my future held, but I did know that I didn't want my life to be bound to something that other people could constantly try to take away.

"I don't want that kind of life," I said.

She frowned and sat back in her throne, a look of disappointment flashing across her face.

"It's my life now," I said softly.

Her kohl-rimmed eyes narrowed, but then she smiled faintly and nodded. "I suppose it is. May your future be as bright and everlasting as the Egyptian sun."

TWENTY-NINE

ere, honey, put on some sunscreen." My mother thrust
a bottle of SPF 30 in my face.

I waved her off. "I need a good tan." I glanced at my
pasty white arm and sighed. Why couldn't I have inherited
Cleopatra's olive skin? My mom put the sunscreen down
next to me with a pointed look. "Fine," I grumbled.

"Nice to see you didn't lose any of your spunk over there
in Egypt," my dad said. He winked at me from behind the
steering wheel of our rented speedboat, then trained his eyes
back on the water.

When I'd gotten back from Egypt, my parents asked
what I wanted to do to celebrate the small victory of, essentially, saving the free world. I told them I wanted to rent a

boat on Lake Monroe. I thought it would be fitting, since Cleopatra and Antony's reign ended with a naval battle.

But my life was just beginning.

Declan had returned home to California, back to school and Hannah. He'd tried to give me a little-sister pat on the head before boarding the plane, but I'd grabbed him in a bear hug and finally heard a normal laugh from him. I watched his plane take off, and was glad he could return to his life. Except it wasn't really the same for him as it was for me. He still had to face the reality that his brother was on the opposite side.

I glanced around at my sisters and smiled, tears in my eyes. They were on my side. They would *always* be on my side.

Slade lightly brushed against my bare shoulder and I shivered. I smiled at him, studying his face. The poison had aged him, brought out lines on his face that weren't there before. He was still struggling to fully regain his shifting powers and strength, which often resulted in him appearing near where he wanted to be, but not exactly. For example, when he'd shifted to meet me that day, he wound up across the street in our neighbor's hot tub instead of in our living room.

"Long-lost loves," Morgana said. She was perched underneath the awning, shielding herself from the sun lest she get any color and not look completely frightening.

"They are," Gia chimed in. Her skin was practically glowing in the sunlight, her blond hair falling around her shoulders like a waterfall.

"Yeah, yeah," I laughed. "Are you going tubing again, G?"

She shook her head. "Taking a break." She sighed. "I miss Zombo."

I nodded sympathetically. Apparently when I destroyed the Book, Zombo had died . . . again. My sisters buried him in the backyard, near Morgana's lilies. My mom promised to get Gia another dog, despite Doppler's loud, wailing protests.

"Ben?" my dad said as he turned to Leah and her boyfriend. Ben had an arm casually slung around her, in that comfortable way they had.

"Sure." Ben stood up, walked to the back of the boat, and jumped on the tube. I looked back at Leah and smiled. I knew she'd done a lot of behind-the-scenes PR work in Inis Mor on my behalf, telling the Créatúir that I wasn't to blame for Slade's poisoning and convincing everyone that our relationship was real.

Not that it mattered. As soon as I got home, I told Slade that he needed to accept the position of king after all. I couldn't let him give that up for me, as much as I wanted him in my world full-time. So we'd worked out a system: since time moves slower in his realm, he would visit as much as he could during their nighttime, and tend to Other Realm business during the day. It wasn't a perfect or even a long-term solution, but it worked.

We laughed as my dad revved the boat, turning sharply until Ben flew off. Then he anchored the boat and kicked back, opening up a bottle of water.

Slade and I walked to the front and sat down, looking out across the sparkling lake. I gazed into the distance and wondered if it truly was all over. If maybe Grant or Paul, or some other group, would rear their scheming heads and want to use me for some other purpose.

As though reading my thoughts, Slade said, "I'll keep you safe."

I smiled. "Thanks, but you know I can take care of myself. I'll keep *you* safe."

"Fair enough."

I leaned my head against him and closed my eyes. Cleopatra may have had gold, jewels, and power in her time, but I had everything in the world.

THE END

About the Author

Maureen Lipinski is the author of women's fiction and young adult books. A graduate of Miami University (in Ohio, not Florida), she lives in the Chicago suburbs with her husband and two children.

For the record, she has no supernatural abilities... that she knows of.